THE SINGULARITY WARS

IN THE SERVICE OF THE GUILD

PAIGE DANIELS

DEDICATION

To family… It isn't always blood. I couldn't have done this without all of you.

CHAPTER ONE

THE ETHOS VIRUS HAS RAVAGED ANOTHER COLONIST OUTPOST ON CORGON-9. THIS IS THE TENTH OUTBREAK ON AN INDEPENDENT PLANET. THE COUNCIL OF INDEPENDENT PLANETS HAS MADE NUMEROUS PLEAS FOR VACCINES FOR THOSE HARDEST HIT, BUT THOSE PLEAS HAVE GONE UN-ANSWERED BY ALL THE KEEPER FACTIONS.

ON THE FLOATING DISPLAY, A lifeless child hangs limply in her mother's arm. The scene unfolding before me elicits the barest hint of remorse for the woman. I click the scene off before I have time to think about the atrocities, then I turn to face the man in the mirror. I brush a few hints of dust off my crisp black uniform then straighten the medals and ribbons adorning the crimson sash hanging across my chest. My hand drifts to my freshly shaved face, and my fingers brush the cherry-red birthmark on my jaw, which is usually hidden by stubble.

Fuckin' formal ceremonies...

I turn away from the mirror and head out of my cramped quarters. I close my eyes and take a deep breath of crisp, clean air then head to the white limestone building in the distance. Footsteps scurrying next to me make me turn around.

An athletically built blond woman in the same uniform as mine, but without the sash and medals, calls to me breathlessly. "Paladin Reece!"

"You're late, kid."

She glances at her comm-tile and looks at me unwaveringly. "I am not. I'm right on time."

The edge of my mouth curls slightly. Plebe Cane is one of the best recruits I have trained and will surely make paladin in record time, but I can't let her know that.

I return her look and growl. "Are you arguing with me, Plebe?"

She stays stock-still and stares right at me. "Sir, no, sir. I will try to be earlier next time."

"Very good. If you're on time, you're late."

Since I'm nearly a foot taller than she, I walk at a quick pace so that she nearly has to run to keep up with me. As I walk, I ask her, "Do you know what we are going to see today?"

"Sir, yes, sir. Paladin Hale is to be relieved of his paladin title. He's now an untouchable, unfit for paladin service because of his betrayal of the Guild."

"Believe everything they tell ya, Plebe?"

"Sir?"

"There are always two sides to every story. Remember that. The Guild is bought and paid for by one Keeper faction or another."

She looks shocked at my frank statement.

"Look, kid, I'm one of the few paladins that'll shoot you straight here, so it'll do you good to listen to my advice. In theory, our services are available to anyone who can afford them, but who in this galaxy can afford our services but the four factions who own all the wormholes?"

She shakes her head and says, "I'm sure there are some independent corporations that could…"

"Eh, in my nearly fifteen years of service, I've seen that maybe twice. Trust me, kid, we're owned by the Keepers. Why do you think the only way to rise to the level of daimyo is to align yourself with a Keeper faction? Sometimes the balance will tip toward one Keeper faction more than others, and therein lies my point. Know who's in charge and stay on their good side."

We stop in a grassy courtyard with a white stone building facing us. Flanking either side of the building are stone stairs that lead up to a quarterdeck. Uniformed people are all gathered around, looking at it, and a low murmur of anticipation runs through the crowd.

I continue on, "Hall was stupid. He pissed off the Liu-Khatri faction. Five of the thirteen elders either are in marriage pacts or have children in marriage pacts with the Liu-Khatri. They'll spin it like he crossed his daimyo, but plenty of people cross their daimyos and don't get more than a few hours of PT."

She gives a wry smile. "Like you? Screwing Daimyo Rone Corbin's wife?"

I should rip her a new one for the familiarity of that remark, but the reminder of shoving it down that ass clown's throat cracks a smile across my face. "First, watch yourself, Plebe. Second, she wasn't his wife at the time. Third, my point exactly. Daimyo Corbin made a pact with the weakest faction at that time because that was all who would take him. No one cared, so I got a few days in the box, and mostly everyone thought it was funny. However, had I done that with a more powerful faction, I wouldn't be talking to you now."

"Sir, I just want to do my job. Politics isn't my thing."

"Me, neither. You see me rushing to make daimyo?"

She shakes her head.

"Right. I got no interest in indenturing myself in a marriage contract or kissing some Keeper's ass for the rest of my life. I just want to go out and execute whatever or whoever they want me to take out. Which brings me to my last bit of advice…"

"Sir?"

I look up at the parade deck, where a man in drab brown clothing is flanked by a man and a woman in uniform. Behind him are thirteen elders dressed in red robes. The crowd goes silent.

I turn to Cane and whisper, "Hale might've been spared with just being busted down to plebe and given a few whacks, but…" I look at the man kneeling before the elders and take a deep breath. "He ran his mouth. It would be one thing to screw up or refuse a run, but to publicly speak against a faction… That's a whole 'nother thing. Keep your mouth shut—do what they tell ya. Kid, it's not a matter of politics. It's a matter of survival."

"Sir, yes, sir."

We're both quiet and turn to watch the scene in front of us. An elder, an old woman with long flowing white hair, steps forward and speaks. Her voice is projected throughout the courtyard.

"Fellow members of the Guild, it is with a heavy heart that I must strip this once-noble paladin of his title. From this day forward, Paladin Hale has never existed in our ranks. There are repercussions for not following orders." Her voice rises to a fever pitch. "We are members of the Guild! We are elite, not some run-of-the-mill mercs. There is honor in our ranks!"

The crowd laughs and cheers. As she closes her eyes and breathes deeply, the crowd silences. She looks at the uniformed people who escorted Hale out and nods.

The man and the woman produce solid-metal batons and without emotion introduce the instruments to Hale's body. Hale makes few sounds as the paladins take turns unleashing the wrath of the elders on him. Slowly, Hale's body slumps to the ground in a puddle of crimson. The crowd's raucous cheers fill the courtyard. I look at my side, and my plebe is joining in the frenzy. I cannot. Hale was an honorable man, just stupid. This is not an honorable way to die. The elders and Keepers are turning the Guild into something it was never meant to be. I heave a sigh. Nothing much I can do, I guess, except serve until I die.

CHAPTER TWO

THE CEREMONY ENDS WITH THE two paladins heaving Hale's body off the quarterdeck. It'll stay in the courtyard for a few hours before a few plebes are dispatched to dispose of it. As everyone files out, I take note of all their faces. They are all much younger than my thirty years. Most everyone my age made daimyo or died years ago. I have no friends. Nobody has friends in the Guild—just those you may trust a little more than others. My body feels every bit of the nearly fifteen years I've served as paladin. On a daily basis, my robotic arm and cybernetic eye cause me pain, my knees ache, and memories...

Plebe Cane's voice breaks my wallowing. "Sir, what are my orders for the day?"

"I looked at your times on sim-training session One Lima Niner, and your stats aren't what they need to be. I want you in that trainer for the remainder of the day. I'll be checking on you at the end of the day, and if you aren't where I want you to be, then prepare yourself for night PT."

She looks at me wide-eyed. "If I may ask, sir, what is the target range I'm aiming for?"

"What fun would it be if I told ya?"

She starts to protest but is stopped by my look.

"I'd get goin', Plebe. You're wasting time."

"Sir, yes, sir."

She runs toward a high-rise glass building in the distance. I smile, remembering my time in simulators. It was absolute hell training in a hot, dark room with a myriad of tactical situations one might encounter as a paladin. What we don't tell the plebes is that most of the situations programmed into the simulators are unsolvable. I start to head to my quarters when I'm stopped by a buzzing at my wrist. I look down at my comm-tile:

DAIMYOS ROAN CORBIN AND WALKER RAINES REQUEST YOUR PRESENCE IN MEETING ROOM A IN FIFTEEN MINUTES.

I barely breathe out the words, "Ah, fuck. What the hell is it now?"

I squirm in my scratchy formal wear. The least they could've done was let me change into more comfortable gear, and given their late appearance, I had more than enough time to change. I know it's just their way of fucking with me. I stretch out in a chair at the side of the conference table, and before I'm able to get too comfortable, a voice rings out.

"Daimyos Corbin and Raines entering the room."

Getting their adjutant to announce them is a fairly douchey move. I slowly rise for my superiors. Two men clad in gray shirts and pants with matching gray jackets adorned in medals and ribbons stand in front of me.

One man in his late forties, with dark hair and round glasses, greets me by shaking my hand. "Paladin Reece, how are you?"

"I'm great, Daimyo Raines."

The other man, too, is in his late forties but has a receding hairline and is much smaller than Daimyo Raines.

"Daimyo Corbin, how is your wife?" I ask.

Corbin's eyes grow wide, and he shouts, "I should send you down the same path as Hale for your insolence!"

I feign a shocked look. "What? I was just asking about the health of your family."

Raines takes an exasperated breath and says, "Both of you stand down."

I shrug. Both the Daimyos sit, and I join them.

Raines continues, "Let's cut to the chase. We need you on a rather sensitive case."

"Yes, sir."

Raines continues, "Do you know the nature of Hale's transgression, Paladin Reece?"

"Sir, I'm not privy to the goings on—"

Both of them give me a cut-the-shit look. They know I've been around long enough to get the real dirt on most situations around here.

I start again. "Hale fucked up a run having to do with the Ethos vaccine. He spoke publicly about his distaste for the Backic faction's policy of withholding vaccines from colonies who needed it most and instead using it to gain votes and power. From what I hear, the votes didn't go so great for the Backics at the latest galactic conference, and that shipment of vaccines was headed to the Liu-Khatri faction, where they were supposed to exchange it for voting seats at the next galactic conference."

Corbin's eyes narrow. "Do you share his views?"

I shrug. "Frankly, I don't give a shit. I don't know any of the colonists. I figure the Keepers have their reason, and it isn't any of my business."

Raines smiles. "Exactly. The Backic faction has a perfectly viable plan for working with the other Keeper factions in releasing the vaccine in a controlled fashion. All will get the vaccine in due time."

Both the Daimyos are grinning from ear to ear, thinking I'm completely snowed by their line of bullshit. The real story is that the Backic faction sells every new batch of the vaccine to the highest bidder. Then whatever Keeper faction wins the bid sells the vaccine at extreme markups, which means the only people able to afford it are the wealthiest and most affluent and never independent colonies. Honestly, I couldn't give two shits. It's the way things have always been and will always be.

I look at the two men and sigh. "So how does this affect me?"

Corbin answers, "Hale was supposed to guard a shipment of vaccines to a Liu Khatri–controlled planet, but instead it was overtaken by the Separatists. The word is that he was in on the heist the whole time."

Raines clicks on his comm-tile, and a picture of a skinny young man floats above the conference-room table. Raines continues, "We've been able to piece together, from intel gathered during Hale's interrogation session, that this man received the shipment and was responsible for hiding the items. We haven't been able to discern where the shipment is being hidden, though."

I lean back in my seat. "So get the man, interrogate him, and get the shipment?"

Corbin shakes his head. "No, just retrieve him and plant a worm on his systems, and we'll take care of the rest."

"I'm more than capable of getting the information I need from him and retrieving your items."

Raines answers, "Believe me: getting this man is going to be more work than you think. Bring him back here, then we'll assess from there."

I narrow my eyes at him, wondering what he's not telling me.

"The information is being sent to your comm-tile. Review it and be ready to leave first thing in the morning."

"Sir, yes, sir."

I stand as both men leave then look at my comm-tile. "Well, fuck me..."

CHAPTER THREE

THIS RUN IS GOING TO take more prep than I thought. I rush across the campus to my quarters to plan this op. No way am I going to have the time to plan this effectively. A bump to my shoulder shakes me from my thoughts. I look up.

Fuck. I don't have time for this.

A man ten years my junior with flecks of silver running through his jet-black hair gives me a lopsided smile, his blue eyes gleaming. "Get a cherry assignment from the Daimyos?"

"None of your business, Tabor."

Though I try to ignore him and continue to my quarters, he stays close like a fly swarming. "You should've given it up a long time ago, old man. This is a young man's game. Sell yourself to one of those Keeper women—or men—and get a nice cushy daimyo job. It ain't too bad of a life."

"Shut up, Tabor."

"Seriously, Reece, just hand this job over to me. I got it from here."

I ramp up my speed a few notches and bump him in the shoulder as I pass him.

This time, Tabor stays behind and laughs as I speed toward my quarters. "Give me a call if you can't figure it out, Reece."

Tabor Gerr has been in the pocket of Daimyo Corbin since Tabor made paladin. Both of them have a grudge against me. I guess I understand Corbin's beef with me, but Tabor's hate for me has mostly stemmed from the fact that Corbin has told him to hate me.

After an invigorating walk across campus to my quarters, my mind is almost clear of the confrontation with Tabor. First thing: ditch the formal wear for my usual attire of cargo pants and a T-shirt. I settle into a worn chair in my tiny quarters then project all the intel the daimyos have given me on my mark and the vaccine into the air.

It looks like Hale was in collusion with the Separatists to get them the vaccine. I shake my head. Hale was stupider than I thought. The Separatists put on a great ruse that they're for the common people and they want to take the down the Keepers to make wormhole transit free for all. However, it's nothing more than another power grab in a disguise of benevolence for the people. Hale was snowed because as soon as the Separatists got the shipment of vaccines, it seems they sold it to Jake Po in exchange for a pretty sum of credits. Jake is a mover and shaker on the black-market scene. He got his start as a hacker, and once he made a good sum there, he branched out into other black-market ventures. Now in his early twenties, he's made a name for himself. He's definitely not up to Keeper status, but he is fairly powerful and protected. Getting to him won't be easy. I can see why they wanted me to just bring him back here for interrogation. Overcoming his security is going to be a trick, and more than likely, the vaccines aren't going to be stored in just one location.

After hours of sifting through data logs, communications, and videos, my body aches, and I can barely keep my eyes open, but I finally come up with a viable plan. Mr. Po splits his time among his residences in each of the galaxies' quadrants. If my hunch is right, he should be in the Alpha Quadrant in the Lyra system in the Persephone colony. It's a run-down shit hole of a planet dedicated to manufacturing and refining fuel for interstellar ships. Looks like this one is still independent. The comm-tile logs I've pulled from various "entertainment" establishments show that Mr. Po is a particular fan of an exclusive gaming club.

Damn gamers...

CHAPTER FOUR

THE PITCH BLACK AND THE cold rain of the planet seep through my being, making my joints ache and freeze. Maybe Tabor was right—I am getting too old for this game. After being in my cramped transport for a week straight while getting here, parts of me I didn't even know existed ache. Trying to put these feelings aside, I pull my trench coat closer to stave off the pelting rain. In the distance, the street glows with the neon hues of blue and red advertising entertainment, drugs, sex, and whatever else the workers can use to forget their pitiful existence for just a few hours. The only thing beautiful about this planet is its name. I've been here a few times, working runs, and it's always the same dump. A foul stench hangs in the air, and a blanket of black haze is floating from the refineries. After scanning the street for a few minutes, I find the place. The sign glows and flickers: Simlife Best VR Experience. I take a breath and head down the street, rain streaming the whole way.

The establishment is crowded and dimly lit in red. To my left is a traditional bar with a few people gathered around, drinking and waiting their turns for the VR pods littering the place. I take comfort in the fact that this place offers shelter from the cold rain. As I make my way to the bar, a man bumps me in the shoulder, barely aware that I'm even there.

I snarl at him and push him away. "Watch it, will ya?"

He doesn't say a word but just floats away as if I weren't even there at all. He must be one of those Blessed freaks who have the power to sense wormholes. Not a one of them is right in the head.

I mutter under my breath, "Fuckin' freak," as I sit at the bar.

I light a cigar and inhale the woody smoke as I survey the lounge. All the egg-shaped VR pods are glowing red and have numbers floating above them, signifying how long their sessions have to go. Nothing seems out of the ordinary just yet, but I haven't really had to time to watch. That's ninety percent of my job: watching, observing, and waiting for a mark to get sloppy. I got all the time in the world. A motorized drone rolls up to me, and I place an order for whatever watered-down shit they have on special. I have to be at the top of my game, but I can't look too obvious, either.

"So what's your favorite VR pastime?" a woman asks in a melodious voice.

I turn in the direction of the voice. A woman is perched on a barstool, dressed in cargo pants, boots, a form fitting T-shirt, and a jacket. As she smiles, her gray eyes sparkle. Her jet-black plait falls off her shoulder with a flick of her head. She lifts an eyebrow, then her almond-shaped eyes narrow as if she's in deep thought.

She continues, "Let me guess... You don't seem like the sort who rides dragons and goes off and has affairs with beautiful elven princesses."

"Look, ma'am, I just found the first bar that had a seat open so I didn't have to wait for a drink."

She wrinkles her nose at my drink. "You call that a drink? That's mostly water." She signals for the waiter-bot and makes an order. It quickly produces a drink, and she puts it in front of me while taking my original drink away. "This will get you where you're going. You can thank me later."

I put the concoction up to my nose and clear my throat. I take a sip, and it burns all the way down. I cough. "Uh, thanks." I turn away from her to put the conversation to an end and start my survey once again.

"You didn't answer my question," she says, cocking her head.

"What question?"

"Uh, what's your favorite VR pastime? By my estimation, you got at least an hour wait for the next available pod." She looks up at the queue list hanging up at the bar. "Is your name up there?"

I grit my teeth. "I told you, ma'am. I just came here to get a drink."

She laughs. "Ma'am? Seriously? My name's Kira Dresden. And you are?"

I slump my shoulders. "Hannibal Reece."

"Really?"

"Really what?"

"Is that really your name? Sounds made up. Maybe I pegged you wrong. Maybe you *are* the type who likes to go off and have kinky sex with elves."

My eyes go wide. "It is my real name. And what the hell is your issue?"

She feigns a hurt look and puts a hand to her chest as if wounded. "Here I am trying to strike up a friendly conversation with you to kill time before your VR session, and all you can do is be mean. I'm hurt."

"Lady—"

"Kira."

I clench my jaw and breathe forcefully out my nose. Usually, I make a point to ensure no collateral damage occurs when I'm taking out a mark, but I might make an exception in her case. "Kira. I just want to have a drink... alone. I thought this would be the place—"

Something's not right here. This woman does not belong in this place. No one in these VR bars strikes up conversations with a stranger. As a matter of fact, the whole reason people come to places like this is to avoid reality. I give her a once-over. Her glowing olive complexion and voluptuous build betray that she hasn't spent a lifetime breathing in toxic refinery fumes.

"What gives? You belong here about as much as I do."

"Ah, you're quick. I got some information I think you might be interested in."

"Doubtful." I turn away from her.

She gets up from her barstool and walks over in front of me. The petite woman scowls and gives me a piercing look. "I'm trying to help you."

"More likely, you're trying to help you."

"Probably, but what do you care if the end result is something that helps both of us?" When I don't turn away, she continues, "You're a paladin, aren't you?"

"Why would you say that?"

"Y'all look the same. Trying to look inconspicuous, but you have the same military pompous-ass air about you. The likes of you don't come into bars like this… ever."

"Let's say I am. So what?"

"Well, Mr. Reece, elf defiler—" When I growl, she laughs. "The only reason I could see that a paladin would *ever* lower themselves to coming into an establishment like this is to find someone high profile. Maybe a certain someone I've been tracking on and off for the last few months—a certain someone who thinks he's a powerful hacker who likes to slum in VR bars, remembering the good ol' days. And maybe this person stiffed me on a fare I'm *still* trying to recoup from. Maybe I know exactly where he is right now. And maybe, just maybe, I have another piece of information you will find interesting."

She has my attention, and I smile. "So… Ms. Kira Pain-in-the-Ass, if you knew of a person like this, why would you ever tell me, and what the hell else do you think would be interesting to me?"

"Well, Mr. Reece, as you probably know, being a possible paladin and all, Mr. Po—" She feigns a shocked look and puts her hand to her mouth and says, "Oopsy, did I say that name out loud? Anyhoo, this man is quite well protected. No way am I getting through his guards alone—a minor tactical error I overlooked."

"Eh, minor. So if I was to help you with a certain someone, what other piece of information do you have for me?"

"Uh, no, you agree to help me get the fucker."

"That's where we're going to have a problem. My bosses want to have a word with him. No way you can have him."

"Silly paladin, I don't want him. Just access to his comm-tile for like five minutes… tops. I can get my due and get the hell out of here."

I'm silent for a few seconds. The whole time, she looks at me patiently, waiting for my response. I size her up and decide it's worth the risk of the partnership. I've entered riskier partnerships to get a mark.

I extend my hand. "Fine. You can have his comm-tile forever as far as I'm concerned. So what's the other piece of information?

She looks over my head and says, "I'm pretty sure that dude skulking about over there is another paladin looking for our mark."

I turn around.

Fucking Tabor!

CHAPTER FIVE

"**S**o I guess I was right, then," Kira says. "When did he come in?"

She shrugs then takes the drink she ordered for me and gulps it down in a single breath without even flinching. "Not long before you, but he wasn't very subtle, like you were. He just started rummaging through pods. I didn't even have a chance to try and make a deal with him."

"Hmph. What a shame. Now, you're stuck with me."

She screws up her mouth and shrugs. "Eh, you seem like you might have a few more years of experience and aren't a total dumb ass like him. He's never gonna find what he's looking for out in plain sight."

"Thanks. I think."

Silent, I look at Tabor off in the distance, searching from pod to pod. Sure as hell, Daimyo Corbin gave him a heads up on my mission in hopes that Tabor would swoop in and make a fool of me.

Fuckin' Corbin!

I look over at Kira, who is now pounding her second gut-fire drink. *Blast. I'm stuck here on a backward planet with a flippin' boozehound independent transporter—or is she a merc—as a partner?*

"So what's your deal? You an independent transporter, a merc, or what?"

She laughs. "Not a merc, m'dear. Just an independent transporter. Like I said, Mr. Po put out feelers for some shit. I got it for him. He didn't pay on the agreed terms. I just want my due. So what's the plan, Mr. Reece?"

"As much as I want to beat that fuckface Tabor into oblivion, the smart plan is to get to where Mr. Po is hiding out, get in, and get out." I'm silent for a second as I gather my thoughts. "What's his security detail look like?"

She sidles close to me then makes a few swipes and pushes on her comm-tile, and a picture of Jake Po surrounded by an entourage appears. She points at two big guys. "Obviously, these two guys are going to be pretty tough opponents, and that's his first line of defense." She swipes a few more times, and a picture of three leggy, beautiful women is displayed.

A grunt emanates from me.

"Yeah, I know. They're hot. But my gut tells me they're more than just a few pretty faces."

"Your gut is probably right. So you have any weapons on you?"

She cocks her head then discreetly opens her jacket to display a disrupter pistol. "Please."

I'm starting to like this woman more and more. "You know how to use flash bangs?"

"I'm pretty sure I can figure it out."

"All right then. What pod is he in?"

"Oh, he wouldn't use anything here in gen-pop. There's a few private rooms in back for VIPs." She nods toward Tabor in the distance. "Luckily, your friend hasn't figured that out yet."

"He's no friend of mine."

"Hmph. Maybe you can tell me the story later."

"Well, if all goes as planned, there won't be a later. I'll have my man, and you'll have your comm-tile, and we can go our separate ways."

She gets a sneaky smirk on her face. "That's a shame. We were just starting to have fun. Thought maybe we could have more fun after this was over." She gives me a wink.

That must be the two drinks she pounded down.

Without missing a beat, she quickly turns the subject of the conversation. "So the VIP room is in back. Problem is I don't know which room is his. Fortunately, the VIPs warrant better service than the waiter drones. Maybe if we—"

I smile and finish her thought. "Find a few uniforms and take some orders?"

"You know, I don't care what they say about you paladin. You're okay, Mr. Reece." She points her head in the direction of a doorway that reads Employees Only over the entrance. "After you."

In the back, a few people are too busy to notice us working our way to the locker room. Once there, we look around and find a few uniforms that might fit us. Finding clothes that will fit my larger-than-average size is always a challenge, but I'll make these work. I swivel around to find some private accommodations to change but find none. When I turn back around, Kira already has her shirt over her head, exposing her barely covered breasts.

She pulls her shirt off all the way and smiles. "Shy? Do you need some privacy?"

"Of course not."

As I undress, I can't help but steal a few looks at her. She's very curvaceous and quite beautiful when she shuts her mouth. Most of the women I'm exposed to in the Guild are more athletic and harder, the exact opposite of Kira. Fraternization is discouraged between paladins. It certainly does happen from time to time, but mostly it's just business. In my case, there's never been anyone I felt particularly motivated enough to break the rules for. But this woman... is like a breath of fresh air.

Rein it in, Reece. When this is over, you won't see her again.

Once dressed, she heads over to me and tugs at the tight uniform. "Don't quite make these to fit big guys like you. C'mon, let's get goin'."

When we head back out of the area, I grab a few trays of snacks and booze to complete the charade. She points toward a bank of rooms behind the pods, and we head toward them. While we traverse the pods, I keep a look out for Tabor, but I don't see him. With any luck, he hasn't discovered this bank of rooms yet. After a few minutes, we're finally in a corridor lit only by a black light. Our white uniform jumpsuits glow an eerie blue. I start to knock on the first door, but then I'm stopped.

Kira gasps, "I think we have a problem."

I look over, and Tabor is standing over Kira with a knife pressed against her back. She gasps and struggles.

He laughs as he says, "My, she is a pretty one. Wanna take her back to my ship and take turns?"

I growl at Tabor. He's a sick son of a bitch. I know plenty paladins who get a thrill out of raping and torturing, but I've always been more the type to just get the job done and move to the next one.

I take a breath to calm myself and keep from doing anything too rash. "Put the damn knife down. What the hell are you doing here, Tabor?"

"Just keepin' an eye on you in case you fuck up the job, which looks like you're right on track to do."

"I'm doing just fine. Put the knife down and—"

I'm cut off by the sound of Tabor yelling in response to Kira slamming her heel into the top of Tabor's foot. She backs away from him, but his reach is long enough to grab her and throw her into a wall. As she slides down the wall, I head for Tabor, but I'm stopped by the sound of a few doors opening to see what the commotion is about. Through one of the doors, I see him, Jake Po—he's looking wide-eyed at the melee.

When I start toward the little man, a large guard cuts me off and yells, "Get him out of here!"

Two women yank Po out of his seat while I'm restrained by the guard, and they disappear behind a hidden door in the room. The large guard slams me hard against a wall and is off with the rest of the entourage.

Kira shrieks, "No! What have you done, Tabor? We had him!"

She starts after Po, but Tabor takes his knife and shoves it into Kira's side. She crumples in a pile.

Tabor gives me an evil smile. "Have fun cleaning up that mess. I'm gonna get me a mark." He's off in an instant.

I look down at the motionless woman, wondering what to do.

CHAPTER SIX

I KNEEL DOWN NEXT TO KIRA. She's alive, but her blood is flowing profusely. I take her pulse, and it seems strong and steady. No one who can help is around, and I imagine on this world it'll take forever for her to get treated. I can fix this wound fairly easily on my ship. Last damn thing I need is a tagalong, but maybe she'll have more intel. At this last thought, I scoop the woman up in my arms and mutter a curse. Hopefully, Tabor won't be able to track Po, and I'll be able to blame this fuckup on him. Screwing up another paladin's assignment is grounds for a few weeks in the box and maybe even never being able to make daimyo. Seeing him endure that might be worth all this shit.

Once back on my small ship, I lay Kira on my bunk and simultaneously call out to the computer, "Execute launch protocol Alpha One Gamma. Search for Paladin Gerr's ship and report to me immediately when you lock on him."

The computer responds, "Affirmative, Paladin Reece."

When I look down at Kira, she's regained consciousness. She croaks out, "Hell of a way to get me in your bed. You're pretty cute. If you'd asked nicely, there's a good chance I would've gone."

"Shut up."

She smiles and winces.

I call to the computer as we buck wildly through the atmosphere, "Send a message to Daimyo Corbin and ask him what the fuck is going on. While you're at it, send the same message to Daimyo Raines."

Kira's breath is labored, and her face is drenched in sweat. She lifts her arm and positions her comm-tile where she can see it and swipes and clicks. "I figure since you saved my ass, I could give you all the intel I have on Po. There should be some intel on his ship's call signatures. Maybe run this through your computer and see if they ping on anything."

I smile. "Well, I might not be too sorry I saved your ass now." I say to the computer, "Scan files from Kira Dresden's comm-tile. Scan for comms within given parameters for Jake Po. Tell me if you get any hits."

"Affirmative, Paladin Reece."

Without thinking, I go to a set of drawers in the wall next to my bunk and pull out a medic box. Her once-white jumpsuit is now stained red through the middle. I zip the suit down to her waist, and she wiggles out of the arms to reveal a gaping wound on her side.

I whisper almost to myself, "It looks like he missed any vital organs, so that's good."

"So you have a medical degree or something?" she asks snarkily.

"No, we're all given basic anatomy and medic courses so we can do rudimentary triage in the field and—"

"To make you more lethal killers."

I press gauze to her wound as she winces. "Yeah, so you can bet that he meant to keep you alive. Probably to slow me down." I take her hand and guide it down to the wound and say, "Here—press hard here."

"Then you probably should've left me."

I rummage through the medic box and find a few bottles and tubes then put them to her side. I lift up her hand and the gauze, and the gash oozes. I grab the first vial and give it a good shake. "I thought that you might have good intel on Po, and it might give me a leg up on Tabor. Looks like I was right." I position the vial over her wound and continue, "This might sting a little, but it will keep it from becoming a festering wound and you from becoming a bigger pain in the ass than you already are."

She barely gasps as I pour antiseptic on her cut. I find a tube and apply a thin bead of gel from it down the length of her wound then press the sides together. I finish up by wiping the area clean, and I don't see any leakage from the wound site.

"I think you're going to live." I help her sit up. "That wound sealant has some nerve blockers in it. You need anything else for the pain?"

She lays her head back and closes her eyes. "I could really use a stiff drink."

"Sorry. This is a dry boat. Got to be at peak performance when doing a run."

She curls up her nose. "You damn paladins suck all the fun out of life." She takes a few breaths, closes her eyes, and puts her hand gently on her middle. "I'll be fine. It's actually not that bad now."

I get up and rummage through another set of drawers next to my bunk and pull out some clothes. "I'm goin' to the head to change out of this ridiculous uniform."

Before I turn to go, she asks, "Hey, you got a spare shirt? I mean unless you want to stare at me with my tits hanging out."

I scour through my meager belongings and find a shirt. I start to throw it to her but then hold back. "Hmm, I do like this view, though."

She laughs. "Just give me the shirt, perv."

I throw her the shirt and go to the cramped hygiene closet. These Scout-class Scimitars are meant to fit only one paladin somewhat comfortably and one prisoner uncomfortably. Changing in the hygiene closet takes quite a bit of maneuvering and bending in ways my body wasn't meant to bend. While changing, I think about my accidental crew member, wondering what her deal is. There has to be something more to the story than Po stiffing her on a fare. This seems like a hell of a lot of trouble to go to for a deal gone bad. Then again, she's smart, and though she looks to be maybe in her late twenties to early thirties, most independent transporters start fairly young. From everything I've seen, she's savvy enough to know when a fare is worth chasing.

Once out of the head, I throw the uniform onto a small couch across from the bunk. Kira has her eyes shut and is breathing slowly. I cover her with a wool blanket lying at her feet then head to the cockpit of the ship to check for any comm activity—nothing from the daimyos. I look at my nav charts and sensor screens—no hits on Gerr or Po.

Damn.

I stare out into the distance, trying to think of a plan. Failure is not an option, especially if Tabor is still on the case. There's a good chance the daimyos put Tabor on this case to test me. My stomach knots and churns as I think of all the possibilities.

The sound of boots clanking on the metal floor draws my attention from the din of thoughts rushing through my mind. *Jeez, can't that woman give it a rest for a minute?*

I yell back, "There's some electrolyte replacement in the fridge by the couch. They suck, but it'll do you some good to drink one."

In a few moments, I feel a cool hand on my neck and shoulders. She pulls herself close to me so that she can see my console over my shoulder. My heart beats faster, and I close my eyes to will it to slow down, but it's no use.

"Anything yet?" she asks.

"Nada. Looks like we're in this for the long haul." I clear my throat. "I mean, uh, *I* am, at least. I have to stay out here until either I find Tabor or Po or the daimyos answer my call. I can't go back empty-handed without permission." I sigh and rub my temples. "I can drop you where you want. It's going to take me a while to figure out next steps when none of my superiors are answering my damn calls!" I flop back in my seat, the weight of all that has transpired weighing heavily on me. I need to find this mark.

She whispers in my ear, "You always do what you're told?"

I close my eyes and shiver at her breath on my neck. I grunt, trying my damnedest to ignore this woman. "Mostly, that's what paladins do: execute orders."

She playfully rubs my shoulders and whispers in my ear again, "I don't know. You don't seem like Tabor. You think things through more. They don't like that, do they?"

I squirm in my seat and attempt to change the subject. "So you want me to drop you back on Persephone to get your ship? We're just over an hour out of orbit. It won't be any trouble to take you back."

"Why, Mr. Reece, are you trying to get rid of me?"

"No." *Yes.*

"Eh, I think you might need me. So I'll stay put for a while."

"Need you?"

Her playful massage becomes more intense. Despite myself, I start to relax in her hands. She says, "They don't let you guys have much fun. Do they?"

I clear my throat. "We're allowed recreational activities whenever we want."

"Uh-huh. I'm sure all you're able to fit in between runs is a few quick screws with paladin-screened courtesans. That's no fun." She pulls herself in closer and brushes her lips against my neck. "Damn, Reece, you're so tight you're gonna break something. Those courtesans haven't been doing their job. That's for sure."

She's actually not wrong. Forcing words out of my mouth takes all my strength. "Kira, why are you doing this? I could be some sick perv. You don't know me."

She lifts her hands from my neck. I kick myself for saying anything at all, then her warm round ass lands squarely on my lap. She turns to face me.

While her hips make tiny movements on my lap, she says, "I don't know—I think we're pretty similar. And I figured if you were some sick perv, you would've been on top of me, doing what you wanted, when I was passed out on your bunk and not covering me up with a blanket then offering me electrolyte replacement." She brushes her lips down my neck. "I'm out here for weeks, sometimes months at a time, alone. When I do get into a way station, I'm mostly surrounded by sicko pervs. Believe me, I know a sicko perv when I see one. You're just an overworked, somewhat heartless merc. That's an altogether different thing." She traces my earlobe with her fingers then lets them flit down my neck. "You, my friend, need to relax. Something will come to you if you just relax." She takes my one good hand and puts it on her right hip then somewhat cautiously reaches for my robotic hand. I start to pull away, but she doesn't relent and puts it on her other hip. Her middle starts to move against mine again.

I can't control the groans that emanate from me. "Kira…"

"I'm not after anything. I gave you access to my comm-tile so you can tell that I'm not hiding anything from you. I just sensed another overworked kindred spirit in you. If you don't want this—"

Before she's able to get the rest of the sentence out, I put my mouth on hers. After a few seconds, I pull away. "I told you there was nothing on the comm report. We're gonna be out here for a while. Might as well do something to kill time."

"That's the spirit, Mr. Reece."

I put my arms around her and lift her out of the chair but not before saying, "Call me Hannibal."

CHAPTER SEVEN

OUR BODIES ARE A TANGLE in the tight confines of my bunk. A desire I didn't even know existed has been sated. She is lying next to me, breathing slowly and quietly. I smile and run my fingers through her ebony locks. Every moment since I was sold to the Guild has been planned and overseen—except this one singular moment with her, the embodiment of chaos. Not even the Guild could harness or predict Kira Dresden. Now I know why they keep such tight reins on us. Her eyes flick open, and she takes my hand and brushes it across her lips.

"So… when should I plan the ceremony?"

My eyes go wide, and my heart beats wildly. "Wh-What are you talking about?"

Her mouth turns down and she swallows hard. "Hannibal, we shared a beautiful time. This was my… my first time. We need to commit ourselves together."

I squirm in the close confines. "Hold on now. I thought—"

She busts out in laughter. "Oh c'mon. Are all paladins so gullible?"

In an instant, my body relaxes, and I push her. "That wasn't funny."

"You didn't see your face. It was hilarious." She untangles herself from me to sit up at my side, and as she does so, she winces. She puts her hands on either side of my face and kisses my lips. "Don't have much of a sense of humor, do you?"

"I do when it's funny."

"Trust me. It was." She arches her back and stretches as I watch in appreciation. She looks me up and down. "Seriously, though, I had fun. After all of this is over, I'll give you my comm signatures. Feel free to catch up with me when you can."

Fun—something I thought I knew about but really didn't until now. All my life with the Guild has been protecting my ass from the likes of Tabor and Daimyo Corbin between doing whatever bidding the daimyos and elders saw fit to give me. The last time I can remember having fun was screwing Daimyo Corbin's wife—not because she was particularly good at it but because I knew it would piss him off. Kira's gray eyes flicker with the promise of something dangerous that's been held from me. I know I'm playing with fire, and I don't care.

"You can count on it," I say. "But for now, I think we need to figure out what the computer's found. It's been chiming for a while now."

"Ugh. I know. Probably about our third or fourth time into it, I heard it go off. I will have to say you do have some stamina, Hannibal."

"Why, thank you, Kira."

She hops out of the bunk and swipes one of my shirts from the floor and throws it over her head. Her hair is a disheveled mess, and she doesn't even bother to straighten it before she heads out to the cockpit. I put on a pair of boxers I find on the floor and head to the cockpit too. I sit in the captain's seat. Instead of sitting in the copilot seat next to me, she settles on my lap.

My hands flit across the console as I say, "Computer, display messages and findings."

The first message is displayed. Daimyo Raines's face is displayed. I hit Play.

"What the actual fuck do you think you're doing out there? You were given orders to execute. How dare you black out your comms for three fucking hours! I don't care what your bullshit excuse is. Get your fucking mark, or there will be hell to pay."

I lift an eyebrow. "Three hours—not too shabby."

She laughs, and I continue with the next video message on queue. This time, Daimyo Corbin's face is displayed, and he's grinning from ear to ear. That smirk makes my stomach drop. This can't be good. I hit Play on my console.

"You fucked yourself good this time. Daimyo Raines is pissed at you. Your stock is plummeting with all the daimyos. My man is on the job, and he has a lead, which should get the job done you failed to do. I'm sure to be the next elder installed now."

I sink back in my seat and groan. Kira screws up her face and says, "So I take it his 'man' is that Tabor guy?"

"Yeah. Now I need a stiff drink."

"What's he mean about your stock plummeting?"

I sit back up and shrug. "Kira, I'm old—"

"Not much older than me."

"No, not really, but for a paladin, I am. I never had much stomach for politics. I love being in the field. I think I would die behind a desk, so I never even considered a run for daimyo. Pretty much, I thought I'd be long dead before now. I think everyone else did too. Now, I've reached an age where I'm viewed as diminishing returns." I lift up my robotic hand and add, "Especially with this thing. So I have to work harder to prove myself on every run. The other choice is go for daimyo, but then I'd need backing by other daimyos, elders, and a Keeper faction. That ain't happening. I guess I should've seen this coming."

Her shoulders slump. "So like, they'll execute you once you reach a certain age?"

I chuckle. "Nothing that obvious. Mostly, they send the older guys on a bullshit run, and maybe there's a ship malfunction or their 'mark' gets the better of them. Everyone knows, but no one talks about it."

"Well, that's bullshit." She gets up from my lap and clicks on the console until Daimyo Corbin's video is displayed again. She looks at it closely, zooming in on sections, studying. Then she says, "That's what I thought I saw. You see it?"

I walk over to her and peer over her shoulder and see a map with a blip on it. "What of it?"

She shakes her head then zooms out and points at the time stamp on the video. "See that? Corbin sent that less than hour ago." She zooms back in on the map. "What's that look like?"

"Tabor!"

A giant smile comes to my face. I can't believe I missed this. That's clearly an icon for a Scimitar. Those ships are used exclusively by paladins on runs.

She continues. "Uh, yeah, Corbin was too stupid to clear his screen behind him. I'd bet you a bag of that electrolyte replacement he was just on his comms with Tabor and called you to gloat."

Her face becomes focused as she clacks and swipes on the console. She looks like a completely different person from the playful smartass I met in the VR bar. A star chart floats in front of her alongside a map, which is an extremely blown-up version of the one behind Corbin. She leans back in her chair and swipes and clicks at her comm-tile. Then she looks back at me. "Look at this. According to my calculations and what I can discern from this shitty picture and your half-assed star charts—and how you even get decent routes with these things is beyond me—is that Tabor is still in Alpha Quadrant. He looks like he's close to a Liu Kahtri hole."

"That is impressive. Where is he going?"

"Yeah, I'm pretty good with charts and calculations. Did you think I was some dingbat screwing random dudes I meet in VR bars?"

"Uh…"

"Best not answer that. In answer to your question: I'm not sure where he's going. Give me a sec to figure out where that hole leads and cross-reference it with known hideouts of Jake Po."

Again, she focuses, intent on a goal. She doesn't speak a word but just looks at her charts and clicks on her tile. Then she looks up at me and says, "Seriously, these charts suck the big one. You care if I upload some decent ones on here? It'll make my job a lot easier."

I wave my hand. "Feel free to do what you need."

"Good man." Again, more silence and calculations. She leans back in her chair and smiles. "Well, fuck me. I know where he's going."

"Where?"

"It has to be the Beta Quadrant, smack dab in the Cygnus system. There's a little shit planet there, where Po got his start. Practically owns the whole fucking planet. He always dodges there when shit gets deep. I should've thought of that in the beginning. I'm so stupid."

"I'd say you're the complete opposite."

"Aw, compliments will go miles in getting you laid again."

"How long to get there? There's no way we're going to beat Tabor to the punch since he's got such a head start on us. We need to figure out a way—"

"Do you trust me?"

I narrow my eyes at her. "I don't trust anyone at all, but since you got skin in the game, I guess I don't totally distrust you."

"I respect that. I'm guessing all your paladin ships have the same shit maps that you had here." She zooms in on a spot in her map, which really is much better than mine. "There's sort of a shortcut here. It doesn't sound like it because we're going to have to traverse a hole that takes us into some backward territories, but there's another hole there that cuts off parsecs from the route he's taking. So if you don't mind, set a course while I'm in back, getting decent."

As she passes me, I grab her around the waist and pull her tight. "I don't know how to thank you."

"I'll show you later." She pats my cheek. "Besides, I couldn't have my favorite lay being executed."

She wiggles free from my grasp and goes back to the head.

CHAPTER EIGHT

KIRA'S CHARTS, NAVIGATION INTUITION, AND calculations all prove to be spot on. We're within a few hundred million klicks of our mark's home planet. We see no sign of Tabor yet, but according to Kira's calculations, we're at least an hour ahead of him if he stayed his course. Po's headquarters is just a few hours away. I look over at Kira, who is perched in the seat next to me. She has a shirt of mine draped over the uniform we took from the VR bar. The top half of the uniform is pulled down to her waist, and she's using the arms as a sort of makeshift belt wrapped around my gigantic shirt. Her hair is now combed and fashioned into a tight plait. She looks much more businesslike now than earlier.

We're both looking at intel we've been able to glean from various sources about Po's planet. There's really not much industry here—just a few of Po's ventures keeping it barely afloat. His compound is extremely locked down since he's a paranoid hacker. Getting in there is going to be nigh on impossible, but they must have one hole in their system, and that's what we're looking for.

After hours of looking at the same data and not finding a damn thing, I need a break. I look over at her and ask, "So what did Po screw you on?"

She stiffens and looks at me. "I told you. I delivered something he requested, and he didn't pay what he promised."

"What did you deliver?"

"What's it matter?"

"Just making conversation."

"Sorry, Hannibal. I like you, but there's some things I keep close.

It's best you don't know much about it. So what are you going after Po for?"

"Same situation as you. I can't talk about."

She shrugs. "I get it. So how often you do runs?"

"As often as possible. I spend more time in this rig than I do my quarters at the Guild. Honestly, I'm fine with that. Too much bullshit going on there. If there was a way I could just float out here and never go back, I'd be fine with that."

"Hmph. Sounds like you're not a typical Guild member, clamoring for the next spot up the rung." She looks me up and down then blurts out, "So how did it happen?" nodding at my robotic arm and eye.

"Actually, it wasn't that long ago. One of our analysts gave me some shit information, and instead of what should've been a simple hit on a lone Separatist, I walked into a whole team of them." I lean back and take a deep breath, remembering the day. "Anyway, I was able to take at least five of them down, but it was just too much. They beat me and left me for dead. Guess I was just too stubborn to die that day."

"Damn… They ever find the guys who did that do you?"

"Oh hell yeah," I say with a smirk. "The Guild would never let a crime against one of its members go unanswered." I decide to turn the line of questioning around on her. "So what about you? How'd you get into the independent business?"

She leans back in her chair and puts her hands behind her head. "My parents were independent transporters. As weird as it sounds, I actually had a pretty happy childhood. They taught me everything I know. I was brought up learning how to hack into systems, scrub identities, pick locks, and pull every kind of grifting scheme there was. Honestly, it was pretty fun. When I was about seventeen, I had enough money to buy my own transport. Mom and Dad gave me a few of their clients and wished me good luck. I see them every so often in various way stations. Sometimes, we have a bite to eat together—sometimes it's just a quick hi and bye. I guess they're really the only people who are somewhat permanent in my life. I keep in touch with who I want to. I like it that way."

Her eyes sparkle as she smiles. I envy her free spirit and the ability to go where she wants when she wants. I also envy her family. I have only vague memories of mine, mostly my mother. Despite having a life nearly opposite mine, here she is, just as walled off and lonely as me.

"So, got any grifting schemes that'll get us into Mr. Po's?"

"Hmm... good idea." She swivels in the chair in silent thought. After a few seconds, her face beams. "Hey, check chatter on the low side. See if they're putting out any solicitations for goods or services."

I smirk. *Damn, this woman is smart.* I click for a while then mutter, "Eh, escort services..."

"Uh, no. It's not like I do that with anyone."

"I feel special now."

"You should."

I keep scrolling then stop. "Got it. Rakali."

She gives a shiver. "Oh crap, I hate those little fuckers. I was transporting some produce to... Hell, I can't remember. Anyway, whole damn ship got infested. Wait, are you saying...?"

I smile. "He hasn't made a call for anything, but I keep getting hits on people down there with vermin issues. How hard would it be to ensure that our friend had some vermin issues too and our pest control company was there to swoop in and save the day?"

"You know, Hannibal, you'd make one hell of an independent transporter. You might want to consider it. Although I'd have to give you some flying lessons."

"What's wrong with the way I fly?"

"You fly like an old woman. Hey, care if I take 'er in? Not like I'll have another chance to fly a Scimitar."

"Be my guest."

Her hand grabs the throttle, and the biggest smile I've seen since I met her comes to her face, and we're off like a shot.

CHAPTER NINE

"**H**OLY SHIT," KIRA SAYS. "THAT was the most fun I've had flying in a long time. It's really too bad those things don't hold any cargo because I'd consider getting one."

"I know. That's about the millionth time you said that."

We're both combing through the woods on the outskirts of the city where Po's compound sits. So far, we have a decent haul of rodents, but we're trying to get as many as possible to cause an immediate call. The forest we're in is cold and damp, but the air is cool and clean. I take a deep breath to take in the fresh air.

Kira wrinkles her nose. "The air smells weird here."

"It's called air that's clean and not filtered through a million scrubbers."

She shrugs. "I spent my whole life on a ship. I've never been on an actual planet for more than a week at a time." She looks around. "I guess I'm supposed to think it's beautiful, but it's just too wide open for me. And smells weird."

I laugh. Out of the corner of my I eye, I see another small, sluggish furry beast. Before I can react, Kira dives and snags it by the scruff of its neck. The rodent squeals as she throws it into our tub.

"So, Hannibal, let's say we get in. Then how are we going to find Po, take down all his guards, then get out with the douche?"

"I'm glad you asked. You have any experience with wiring explosives?"

"What do you think?"

"Well, if you don't mind if a couple of our furry friends are collateral damage, I think I have a plan."

"Ki-Reece Pest Control. How can I help you?"

"Yeah, we have an infestation of rakali here. No one else is answering their comm lines. We need them gone now."

"Yes, sir. Whose residence is this?"

"Jake Po—maybe you're familiar with the name? We need you here ASAP."

"Oh yes, sir. Two of our associates will be out shortly."

"Good. You best make it quick."

Kira clicks at her comm-tile then smiles and says, "So far, so good. Seriously, have you ever thought of becoming an independent transporter?"

For an instant, the thought gives me hope, but I know it can't be. I sigh. "No one ever leaves the Guild alive. But I have to say this is the most fun I've had on a run in a long time."

We're in front of a twelve-foot wrought-iron gate, looking around at the compound. It's really more of an enormous house surrounded by gates and guards than a full-on compound. Kira has her hair up in a ponytail, and her face is smudged with dirt. She still looks pretty cute, though. She gives me a smile, and her beautiful eyes twinkle.

No time for that, Hannibal.

My hand hovers over a buzzer on the front gate. Before I push it, I ask, "You ready for this?"

"Absolutely."

I push the buzzer.

"Can I help you?"

Kira answers, "Ki-Reece Pest Control. We're here about your rodent problem…"

We hear static for a few heartbeats, then the gate whines open.

"Come straight to the first door, and someone will meet you there."

We amble down a cobblestone path lined with trees and flowers.

Kira doesn't seem impressed by the display of vegetation. I, however, take a few seconds to gander at the somewhat pastoral surroundings.

As we're walking, she asks, "Seriously, you can't leave the Guild?"

"Not alive. My parents sold my life."

"Fuckers."

I shrug. "It is what it is, I guess. No one has figured out how to leave alive."

"Shame. You'd make a great associate."

"Nothing saying I can't still. Wouldn't it be great to have a partnership with a member of the Guild?"

She says nothing but smiles and walks ahead of me. In the alcove in front of us is a tall, lanky blond woman with her hair tied up in a bun. She's wearing a crisp suit and has her arms folded in front of her. Kira extends her filthy hand, and the woman curls her nose in disgust and recoils at the thought of touching Kira.

Kira shrugs it off and says, "Hi there. Mary Bland, and that"—she points at me—"is my partner, Louis."

I grunt in the blond woman's general direction. She looks annoyed and disgusted.

Kira continues, "I hear ya have a rakali problem."

The woman sighs. "Yes, and my boss is rather perturbed by this issue. If you can get them cleared out by the end of the day, I'll make it worth your while."

Kira gives a low whistle as she eyes the property. "Welp, I can tell ya it ain't gonna be cheap. See, my associate, Louis, gets pissy if he has to work late." She adds in a whisper to the lady, "You know how them menfolk get so needy." She gives a fake laugh and slaps the blond woman on the back with her dusty paw.

The horrified woman jumps back and clears her throat. "Well, yes, um, what will you need from us?"

Kira shrugs and holds up the cages she has in each hand and says, "Need access to all over the place so we can set traps and get the critters. Other than that, me and Louis got it."

"Well, I don't know if we can give you access to *all* areas…"

Kira gives her a sideways look. "C'mon, boss, we need access to the whole place. Those little vermin can hide anywheres. Just two of 'em can produce something like two hundred young'uns a year." She looks at me. "And I thought we were bad, with our six little ones at home." She then looks at the woman and points at me. "That one there got a hell of an appetite, if you know what I mean. Still won't marry me and make it legit, but what can you do?"

The woman looks exasperated at this point and is willing to give Kira anything she wants just so she'll shut up—a fairly common technique: make the mark uncomfortable so they just cave and give you what you want. Kira is exceptional at the role.

"Fine. Fine. But you'll have to be escorted by our security."

Kira nods. "Oh yeah, sure, sure. I totally understand."

The woman says something into her comm-tile, and a few moments later, two large men appear. "These two gentlemen will escort you through the compound."

"Yes, ma'am. I do appreciate you givin' us the chance at this because our little ones are gonna eat good after tonight." She looks at me and chucks me on the shoulder. "Do well today, and you might just get lucky tonight too."

The woman looks like she's going to vomit and says, "Well, yes. Good luck then."

CHAPTER TEN

W E MEANDER THROUGH THE HALLS of the compound, not seeing anything of importance. The guards are not as fazed by Kira's annoying small talk as blond woman was, so getting past them is going to be quite a bit harder. We're both holding cages with a few rodents we found, walking a few feet behind the security guards.

Kira whispers to me, "You think he's even here?"

"If he's here, we'll find him. You need to be patient."

"That's not one of my virtues."

"I gathered."

One of the guards looks back at us. "What you two talkin' about?"

Kira says, "How he wants this here vermin cooked for supper tonight."

The guard shudders and turns around, eager to leave us to our talking. She is a master at this game.

Kira continues, "You sure this plan's gonna work?"

"Nope, but nothing's ever guaranteed."

"Good point. Ya know, I'm kinda sad that we're parting ways after this."

"I'm sure I'll have a few runs I'll need help with from time to time."

"If this is the way your life goes all the time, you'll damn well need my help." She looks at me and says in a louder voice, "C'mon, Louis, I think I hear a critter this way."

She goes to a closed door with a light glowing underneath. Someone is in there. My heart skips, and I give Kira a look. She nods, knowing exactly what I'm thinking then puts a hand in her pocket. She says to the men, "We need in there."

One of the men growls, "Why in there?"

"Because I hear one of 'em. If you hunted these things as long as me and Louis here, you could hear them from meters away. We got a sixth sense about us."

The guards look at each other and shrug. They crack the door open, and the bigger guard holds up his hand for us to wait.

He cranes his head into the room and says, "Uh, sir, the pest-control people need to check out this room."

My heart skips a beat. This is the room. We're finally here.

There is silence and then a whiny "Fine. If you must, but make it quick."

Kira barges her way into the room. "Oh, I wouldn't dream of inconveniencing you longer than we had to. It's just that these little buggers can hide anywhere. Like, once, me and Louis found one in a toilet, of all things. Can you imagine?"

The room is dark except for floating screens surrounding Po. He's perched in a beanbag chair, transfixed by the screens manipulating lines of code, barely aware of our presence.

I stay close to the guards, and Kira gets closer to Po and continues with her inane small talk. "Yup, we've seen quite an influx of these boogers lately. It's crazy. I don't know what's in the water to make 'em go so wild, but I just know—"

Po cuts her short. "Are you done? I have work to do here."

"Not quite," Kira answers.

In two breaths, she drops the vermin cages and has Po in an arm bar. At the same time, I whip a ceramic knife out of a pocket and slash the bigger guard's throat. The second guard goes for his comm to alert others, but before he's able, I knife him in the jugular. I search both the guards and find a couple guns. I toss one to Kira, who has Po facedown on the floor with her knee in his back.

He squeaks, "I know you. You're the girl who—"

She leans on him harder so he's unable to speak. "That's right, you fuckstick. I'm the girl you cheated. Cheat me, and I screw you." She puts the gun in her back pocket, fishes out a few hand restraints, and zips them onto his wrists.

He squeaks, "Ow! Fine. Fine. What do you want? I'll give it to you."

"It's far past time for negotiations. I'm taking what I want!" Kira roars.

I'm at one of his consoles, clacking away, installing a worm in his system. I look at her and nod. "I got what I need. You good?"

She rips off his comm-tile, puts it in her pocket, then nods. "Yup." She looks down at him. "See, you could've just paid me my due, but now we got a paladin here, and I'm afraid you're going to have to go bye-bye with him."

His eyes grow wide, and he shrinks back from me. "No, no, I didn't do anything."

I take the little man by the scruff of his neck.

"You can't get out of this compound. You might be a paladin, but you can't take down all of my—"

He's silenced by a tranq dart I thrust into his leg. In a few seconds, he's slumped in a pile. I heave the scrawny man up and put him over my shoulder. We make our way down the empty hallway. Kira is ahead with her weapon drawn and motions for us to follow. *Good, no one has been notified so far.* In the distance, daylight glows from a glass door. As we get closer to the exit, the guards milling back and forth become visible. Too many are there for us to take alone. I nod to Kira, and she digs in her pocket, produces a small button, and pushes it, and several explosions go off outside. I laugh, and Kira shakes her head.

"I can't believe that actually worked. I'm impressed."

I say, "You have no faith. Totally worth getting bitten by a few of those rodents while attaching the explosives."

The guards that were milling in front of the door are now gone. Kira waits a few breaths and heads out. She peeks out the door and surveys for a few seconds then signals that the coast is clear. Outside is utter chaos with smoke billowing in the distance and screams echoing through the compound. Kira produces the button again, and a few more explosions sound. She walks quickly toward the exit and stops at the keypad for the gate. I look behind me and see guards approaching while her fingers glide wildly over the keys and her comm-tile.

I bark, "You said getting out would be no problem!"

"You gotta give me a sec."

The guards start shooting in our direction, and one shot grazes my ear.

"Kira!"

Almost on command, the gate opens, and the instant there is a crevice barely wide enough for us to pass through, I throw Po's body across, help Kira through, then wedge my body through. Kira presses her comm-tile, and the gate shuts again. While I'm gathering Po, she presses a few more buttons on her comm-tile, and we run away from the compound. She says in a husky voice, "I scrambled the codes on the gate. It should slow them down, but I'm sure they'll be scaling that wall in just a few." She looks up at a tree. "Look, I'm going to go up that tree and hold them off. You get Dumb Ass to the ship and come get me."

"Kira!"

She's halfway up the tree when she yells down, "Don't argue. You can get Po to your ship much quicker than I could—"

"I know. I was going to say don't shoot to kill. Shoot to wound. They'll slow down, trying to help the injured."

She gives me a knowing nod, and I run toward the ship. In the background, I hear her shots ring out, and a few howls follow. Less than a half a klick, and I'm home free.

But then my shoulder feels like a red-hot rod has been shoved through it. I know that feeling well. I will my legs forward, although all the systems in my body want to shut down. Another shot rings out, and this time, my leg bears the brunt of the pain. I look around, and suddenly he appears.

"Tabor!"

No longer able to control my body, I drop Po and bend at the waist.

Tabor's icy eyes glint as he trains his weapon on me. He clucks his tongue. "Told you that you were gettin' too old to do these runs. I guess it was just your time. If it's any consolation, you'll go out a legend among men, who just had one run where the mark got the better of him."

My stomach turns, and my body feels cold. This was my ticket out. I should've known. "Fuck you. Fuck all of you."

He points the gun at my head. In an instant, I think about my life. I never did anyone one bit of good. I sigh. *It's probably for the best.*

A shot rings out, but it's not me that goes down but Tabor. He's on the ground, not dead but unconscious with a gouge through his face. I'm left breathless at the sight before me.

"What are you slacking for? The guards are heading this way. Let's get the hell out of here!" Kira has Po by the scruff of his shirt and is dragging him across the ground, running toward the ship.

The stars surround us back in the comfort of my ship. As I'm slumped on the couch, Kira is steadfastly attending to the task of mending me. In the background Po is yelling and pleading from the prisoner's quarters. I do my best to block out the whining of the imprisoned man.

Kira stops mending for a few seconds and shouts, "If you don't shut the hell up, I'm going to give you something to be sorry about!"

Thankfully, he shuts up. I keep replaying the incidents that just transpired.

Kira nudges me. "You know, you can say thank you at any point."

"That was supposed to be my exit. I'm supposed to be dead."

"And you're not. You're welcome," she says angrily as she pushes together a wound harder than necessary. "Seriously, I saved your ass out there, and you're just moping. I mean, this could be your chance to leave it all. They think you're dead, and I'm sure those guards will make short work of Tabor, so he won't be able to tell the Guild any differently. I can throw a few clients your way, and—"

I hold up my hand. "Kira, no. Tabor is alive. He's a tough son of a bitch. I'm sure he made it back to his ship in time to get away. It would only be a matter of time before the Guild found me either way. If I bring Po back, then I have a chance to prove to them I can do their fuckin' runs even with a paladin ten years my junior trying to take me down. Once a member of the Guild, always a member."

"Then how much longer before Tabor or some other punk is there to take you down again?"

I shrug. "It's gotta end at some point, I guess."

She gets up from my side. "We all have choices, Hannibal, even you." She puts a hand on her side and closes her eyes. "I think those nerve blockers are starting to wear off." She heaves a deep sigh and runs her hands through her hair.

"Third drawer down on the right. Feel around in the very back."

She narrows her eyes at me then walks over to the drawer and produces a flask. "So this is a dry boat, huh?"

I shrug. "I didn't know you too well then. I think you warrant a swig or two of the good stuff now."

She slumps down by me and takes a long drink. "I have no idea what I delivered to him."

I narrow my eyes in question.

She continues, "Just being straight with you. Sometimes I'm asked to, uh… creatively procure items for customers, but most of the time, it's just making boring ol' deliveries. He didn't tell. I didn't ask. My customers appreciate that of me." She leans her head back on the wall and says with the most humility I think she can muster, "Hannibal, it's mostly about the show. If I let someone get away with screwing me over without some kind of fight, then everyone will think they can bend me over. What we just did will make anyone think twice about screwing me over. So… uh… thanks." She takes another long drink then hands the flask to me.

I start to take a drink, but then I stop and kiss her softly on the lips. "No. Thank you, Kira."

She puts her head on my shoulder, and as I let the elixir warm me all the way through, I put my arm around her.

"It's about time you thanked me, dumb ass."

CHAPTER ELEVEN

"PALADIN REECE, I HAVE TO say since you apprehended Po last year, your record has been exemplary." Daimyo Raines looks at his floating netscreen as he talks to me.

I squirm in the chair across from his desk. All I want to do is get back to my quarters, shower, and sleep for days. The last run was on a sweltering desert planet, and the air in Raines's office feels especially cloying now. However, Raines just had to see me the second I was back.

He continues, "Your last few runs have been remarkable. You really have been putting your nose to the grindstone. I was worried after your hand—"

I sigh as I rub my temples. "With all due respect, sir, I have a raging headache and sand in places there shouldn't be sand, and I'm starving. All I've had for the last three weeks are ration bars. So if you could…"

He smiles and looks away from the screen. "That's what I like about you, Reece: you get right to the point." He pauses for a few seconds as if to carefully calculate what he's going to say next. "Do you remember that run last year where you found Jake Po and gave us access to his systems?"

I blurt out, "Oh, the one where everyone marked me for death? Yeah, I recall that."

Raines clears his throat and squirms uneasily in his seat. "Well, yes, not all of us were on board with that plan. As you know, Tabor was put before the Council of Elders for his actions. A few months in the box—and his ability to make daimyo on the line—should adjust his attitude."

I mumble, "I'm skeptical. So the point is?"

"From the worm you planted, we were able to ascertain where Po hid the vaccines. We were able to get a significant portion of them back. However, it seems we're starting to get pings that the vaccine is being made available here and there in limited quantities. We'll hear reports and then months later nothing, then something will pop up again. We need to find the source of this."

I sigh. "Seriously? Why even bother? It can't be that much vaccine. A few common folk get cured—everyone's happy."

Raines clenches his jaw and pounds his fists on the desk. "Everyone is not happy. Backic is hungry to make alliances and rise among the ranks of the Keepers. As you know, that stock was promised to the Liu-Khatri faction, which they were going to exchange for voting seats at the Galactic Conference next quarter. The way things are going, the Backics are going be behind in votes to even the Council of Independent Planets if significant strides aren't made. One such stride would be finding the store of vaccines and whoever is distributing them. I have some information on the latest leak. I doubt this person is responsible for all the leaks, but finding them would be a step in the right direction."

I'm exhausted to the core of my being, not only physically but also mentally, from all the political-grandstanding bullshit. It doesn't matter because in another year or two, Backic will have more votes on the Council than anyone, and the lead faction will be at the bottom, scrounging their way to the top. It never ends. I want to tell him where to shove this job, but I also know escaping Tabor last year put me on thin ice with everyone. On the plus side, this means I don't have to spend any longer on this planet than I have to and maybe I can spend my time with more desirable people.

My shoulders almost slump involuntarily when I say, "I'll get on it immediately, sir."

I start to stand, but Raines stops me by holding up his hand. "That wasn't the only thing. I have one more thing I want to talk to you about."

"Sir?"

"I know that you've never been big on a run for daimyo." When I start to retort, he stops me. "Hear me out. If you find who's stealing the vaccine, an alliance with the Backic faction will be a guarantee for you. Councilman Rey is looking for a strong marriage contract for his daughter, Helena." He makes a few clicks on his comm-tile, and a picture of a statuesque blond woman who looks to be in her late twenties is displayed. She is attractive enough but not really my type. Raines says, "She is a shrewd businesswoman who is poised to take the next seat on her faction's council. Having a marriage contract with a council member will be a great boon to your career."

I groan. "Sir, I just don't know…"

His face grows somber, and he says, "Reece, I've been on that side of the desk before. I know looking over here with marriage contracts and a desk job seems like you're ending your life, but it really couldn't be further from the truth. The marriage thing is no big deal in our house. She goes her way, and I go mine. As you know, we daimyos do occasionally go out on runs. It's not a bad life."

"It's just that. I don't know."

"I need to add one other thing. You know that Daimyo Corbin is gunning for you. If you stay a paladin, he will eventually get you. He's pissed half of the daimyos off with his impetuous ways, but the other half stand with him. If you're able to make an alliance with Backic and—" He stops and composes himself. "Well, I don't have to finish that." He looks me up and down. "You're exhausted and not really in any shape to make any good decisions right now. Get back with me after your run. But before that, take care of yourself. I'm going to put in for extra rations for you at the chow hall and a chit to see the courtesans so they can work out some of your kinks."

I stand up and shrug. "I'll take you up on the extra rations, but I'm not really in the mood for courtesans right now. I just want to sleep."

As I head to the door, something comes to mind. It's kind of a ballsy move to ask, but Raines seems to really be courting me to consider the daimyo job, so it won't hurt.

"Sir, I've been going from run to run nonstop for more than a year. Once I find this guy, would you consider a few days leave? It's been over two years since I've taken any."

Raines looks at his comm-tile. "Yes, so I see. Permission granted. Anything in particular you're going to do?"

I shrug. "Nah. Just going to relax."

"I see. Good luck on your run, and enjoy your leave."

"Yes, sir."

CHAPTER TWELVE

A HOT MEAL AND A COOL shower went miles toward muting the aches and pains coursing through my body. Once in my quarters, I turn the thermostat way down and slink in my chair to take in the crisp air. After a few minutes of snoozing in my soft chair, I wake and start combing through all the records Daimyo Raines sent me. He's right—there is definitely a periodicity in when the vaccines are released to the public. More than likely, one or more of Po's guards or associates knew where a stash was hidden and was able swoop in and get it before our guys happened upon it. I have to say whoever it is, is pretty smart. No one site has gotten a lot of the vaccine but just enough to make someone a nice little payday when they needed it here and there—not enough that it would set off any alarms to close acquaintances. I do some more digging and find that the vaccine is usually made available via online auction sites and always by a different username. After the acquisition is complete, all traces of the seller are deleted into thin air.

Jeez, and just when I thought I'd be able to get some time for extra sleep.

The minutes turn into hours combing through the morass of algorithms and cyphers. One after another, all the usernames come up in dead ends. Then I happen on it: Funkcat. This guy can't seem to cover his tracks worth shit. I hit one hub after another, and after nearly twenty-four hours awake, I find a real name: Jordan Burnes, independent transporter and hacker. *Gotcha, ya little prick!* Now, I need to figure out some intel on this guy. Only one person has her finger on the pulse of all independent transporters.

I punch a few numbers into my comm-tile, and it chirps. I let it ring as I go to my fridge and get a well-deserved beer. Finally, the comm-tile stops ringing, and a woman with her ebony locks in a tangle answers. She scowls and is silent for a few seconds. "What the actual fuck are you doing, calling me at this hour?"

"What? It's a perfectly respectable morning hour here," I say, needling her even more.

"Fuck off, Reece. Call me later. It's the middle of my sleep cycle."

"Now, is that how you talk to the man who got you a couple of sweet fares a few months ago?" I swipe the tile so that the display is expanded and floating in the middle of the room then take a sip of my beer as the woman rubs her eyes and stretches.

"I do thank you for those, but if you think that earns you the right to disturb my beauty rest, you're sadly mistaken." She quickly changes the subject. "Wait, it's morning there? So why are you drinking a beer?"

"Your boozy ways have rubbed off on me."

"Good to hear. How'd your run on that sand hellhole go?"

"It was brutal, but I got my man." I squirm in my seat. "I need your help."

"Figures."

"Listen, this is big. I need some intel on an independent transporter."

Kira leans over, and a light fills up her room. She squints and smooths her hair back from her face. She's wearing a tank top with scant panties, which makes me smile. She asks, "Do you have me on the blown-up floating display in your room again?"

"Nope, not me."

"Blast it, Hannibal!"

I laugh at her, which serves to frustrate her even more.

She sighs. "Seriously, why are you asking me for intel on another transporter? We have strict codes—"

"Yes, to undercut each other's fees and screw each other the first chance you get."

She rolls her eyes. "It's different with each other, but selling someone out to the Guild might get a few stern looks, depending on how much the going rate was… How much is the going rate?"

I take a sip of the beer, knowing that I have her. "How about free transit at any of the Backic's wormholes for a month?"

She's silent as she bites her lip and narrows her eyes—the same look she always gets when she's calculating costs or risks. "Who's the guy or gal? You tell me, and I'll tell you if it's worth it."

"Goes by the name of Jordan Burnes."

At that, she nearly leaps out of her bunk. "Oh shit, yes. I would've done that for free."

"Well then…"

She shakes her head. "Oh, no way. You made a deal."

"Fine. Transferring certs your way. Talk, Dresden."

She sits up in bed and flings her hair over a shoulder then roots around in her bunk and produces a hair tie. She puts her hair up in a messy ponytail. Her eyes sparkle as she starts to talk. "First of all, I have no bones at all about selling out fuck-face Burnes. He likes to act like he's an Independent, but he's a Separatist."

"Shit. I don't think those fuckers are ever going away."

"No, and you can tell your pals at the Guild I said this, but they are long past wishing this problem with the Separatists away. They're getting quite the following out there. Promising free hole transit for all is very tempting."

I gulp the last bit of my beer. "You and I both know they're full of shit."

"True, but not everyone else does. But back to Burnes—he has a few main hangouts. I'll comm you those details. Anything he's stolen from you and yours, you'll be able to find at either of those places. Seriously, he's not that smart."

"I kinda gathered."

She stretches and yawns, and a little snippet of her belly shows, which fills me with longing. "So if that's all, I'll be going back to sleep."

She starts to turn off the video, and I say, "No, wait."

She gives me a sideways look.

My stomach knots and turns. I've seen her in person a few times since we first met, and we talk all the time via VidLink, but this is the first time I'm suggesting getting together outside of business purposes.

50

I have no idea how she'll take the idea of hanging out with me for a few days. I shake it off. *It's just for fun, Hannibal. Nut up or shut up.*

I huff out a breath. "Looks like I've been doing such a bang-up job with all these runs lately, they decided to give me a couple of days of leave. Barring you didn't give me shit data, where are you going to be in a day or two?"

Her face beams, then she quickly bites her lip and forces her face to a frown. "I didn't give you shit data. If you want to find me, it should be easy enough."

The video goes dark, and I smile.

CHAPTER THIRTEEN

THE CONFINES OF THE DARK, narrow hallway close in on me. Barely any air flows here, and sweat beads at my forehead. All the places Kira gave me to check came up empty. This is my last-ditch hope. Otherwise, it's back to stalking all his other hideouts and comms traffic until I find something, and who knows how the hell long that could take. I take a deep breath, steadying myself as we walk down the hall. When I look over my shoulder, Plebe Cane is on edge, following my every move. I smirk, thinking about what it was like going on my first real run. She's more than ready for this, and if she doesn't totally screw this up, I'm going to recommend her to run the Crucible to test for the rank of paladin by the end of this month.

I say in a harsh whisper, "Listen, Plebe, I'm going to that room there on the right, the one with the light on. We've checked the whole building, and that's the only way out. Do you remember what Burnes looks like?"

She whispers back, "Sir, yes, sir. I've burned that image on my brain."

"Good. I'm going to flush them out. When you see Burnes, you take him down. I will hold off the others. Look for Burnes and detain him. Got it?"

With her body stock straight and jaw clenched, she gives a curt nod.

I slam on the door with my fist and yell, "I'm looking for Jordan Burnes! Turn him over, and the rest of you can go free!"

Behind the door is clamoring and screaming, then a stream of people run out of the room. Cane's eyes go wide, scanning the mass of people exiting. I slam those that I can into a wall. I look over at Cane, and she has a scrawny man in an arm bar, smashed up against the wall. I pray she grabbed the right man and didn't flip out and grab the first person available. I walk up to the man and do a scan of him. Sure enough, it's him. My heart leaps.

Cane and I are sitting at the console of my ship.

"Listen to me, Cane. Go straight to the Guild and drop him off. Don't let him talk you into making any stops. Just go. I plotted a course on good maps. It shouldn't take you more than a day to get there."

She smiles. "Sir, I got it. You told me you paid my fares at all the wormholes and showed me the course ten times. I'll be fine."

"Hmph, I guess you will be. You did really good, kid. I'm going to recommend you run the Crucible at the end of this month, so I'd spend every waking minute in that trainer if I were you."

Her face brightens and beams. She nods vigorously. "Thank you, sir. I... I..." Her face scrunches up. "Are you sure I can't give you a ride to wherever you're going?"

"Nope. Got my fare lined out. I'll get back to the Guild, no problems."

She smiles. "Going to see your girlfriend?"

"Shut it, Plebe. She's not my girlfriend. She was an integral part of us obtaining Burnes. I need to debrief her on our findings."

"Uh-huh, and you can give me however many demerits you want for this statement, but bullshit." She pushes a few buttons on the console, and the door of the ship opens. "Better go meet your fare. I got it from here, sir."

"You message my comm-tile as soon as you get to the Guild," I say as I back off the ship.

She pushes a few more buttons, and the doors start to close. "Sir, yes, sir. You enjoy your time with your girlfriend."

"Plebe!"

Smoke hangs low in the dark, musty bar, the din of voices, fighting, and music surrounding me. A half smile perches on my face. This is exactly the kind of place Kira loves. I scan the establishment for a familiar face, but I don't see anyone. I sigh and go to the bar and order a drink then mill my way through the establishment. Then I hear a familiar laugh, and I'm pulled to it almost involuntarily. At a table is a gathering of people: big muscular women, beautiful buxom women, old men, young men—they're all here, gathered around, laughing and sharing stories.

A voice rings out among all the others: "Yes, it is true! We seriously taped explosives to bunch of rakali. *And* it worked."

A muscular bald man grumbles, "Bullshit. Like a paladin formed an alliance with you, Kira."

"I'm not lying, Kylin."

"Kira, you've always been full of shit!"

I chime in, "That is true, but not in this case."

As the whole table looks at me, she smiles. "I told you, Kylin." She stands and motions for me to come and sit next to her then motions for the waitress to get me a drink. She holds my robotic hand and nestles her head against my shoulder. She looks at Kylin. "You have anything else you want to say about my story?"

The man holds up a hand and shakes his head. "Nope. You got me, Kira."

In a few minutes, the waitress has another drink in my hand. I take a healthy sip, and all the tension leaves my body.

Kira looks up at me and whispers, "It's good to see you, like for real."

I lean down and kiss her on the lips slowly at first then more feverishly. The whole table whoops and hollers. She pulls away from me, blushing. This is the first time I've ever seen her blush. She grabs my hand and again nestles her head into my shoulder.

Then she talks to the table again. "So like I said, we were at this compound. There had to be at least…" She looks at me. "What would you say? A hundred guards?"

"Oh, at least."

"Right, and I didn't think Hannibal's plan had any chance of working." Her hand leaves my hand and finds my knee then creeps up higher.

I smile at her, and she returns my smile.

"So how did you get this idea, dear?" she asks.

"Well, back on a run on…"

CHAPTER FOURTEEN

HER BODY NESTLES CLOSER TO me, and she's breathing heavily with anticipation and desire. I can't remember if I've ever wanted anything so much as this one moment, this one person. Her lips meet mine and breathe life into my being. My hand traces the curve of her writhing body. She is soft and warm. She is my home. Slowly and gently, I trace the inside of her thigh, and she gasps and smiles. Her body sways and arches in a hypnotic dance. I love to take all of it in—her body, her smell, her energy. Right as she murmurs a plea for me, I put my mouth to hers. Her hands tremble along my chest and dance along my scars, and her arms engulf me, forcing me onto my back. Our bodies are one now, dancing to an unknown beat that only we can hear. Her eyes meet mine, and I'm lost in them. She has me, and she knows I'm all hers at this very moment.

Our bodies collapse in a heap. I'm exhausted and satisfied to my core. Before my eyes shut and the darkness takes over, I breathe out, "My God, I missed you, Kira."

She turns to me and smiles and wraps her arms around me, and her eyes flutter shut. I want to look at her more, but the darkness wins.

I'm awakened by fingers fluttering along my chest. My body involuntarily shudders, and I smile at the beauty at my side.

She stretches and says, "Hey, Sleeping Beauty, you hungry?"

I sit up on the makeshift bed on the floor we fashioned out of blankets and pillows. Her bunk was way too cramped for me, much less the both of us. I look around her quarters, which are small and sparsely furnished with a small bunk and a desk built into a wall, littered with paperwork, electronics, and various parts that need to be repaired. We didn't spend much time at the bar but headed straight for her small Goddard-class freighter and, in her words, "took off for nowhere."

"Famished." I look outside our window, where a nebula pulsates in a colorful display. "Hell of a view."

She grabs a few items from a small fridge under her desk and comes back to our bed. She hands me a ration bar, an electrolyte-replacement bag, and a...

I narrow my eyes. "Is this real fruit?"

She giggles and takes a big bite of the red sphere. She says around it, "Yup. Bartered for it on my last run. I thought, with you coming aboard, I could use some more food."

I eye it appreciatively before taking a bite. Getting real unsynthesized food is a rarity. "This had to set you back a few credits."

She gives me a peck on the cheek. "You might be worth it."

Before I have a chance to take a bite, my comm-tile rings. I fumble through the sheets to find it. A message pops up.

MADE IT BACK TO THE GUILD, SIR. OUR MARK IS IN CUSTODY BEING QUESTIONED AS I TYPE.

GOOD. NOW GET TO WORK ON THE TRAINER.

ABOUT THAT, SIR, THEY WANT ME TO RUN THE CRUCIBLE TOMORROW. SIR, I'M NOT READY.

ARE YOU SAYING THAT MY TRAINING WASN'T SUFFICIENT? THAT A FEW DAYS WAS REALLY GOING TO MAKE A DIFFERENCE IN YEARS OF TRAINING?

NO, SIR.

THEN SHUT THE FUCK UP AND GO PASS THE CRUCIBLE TOMORROW.

SIR, YES, SIR.

GET SOME SLEEP. YOU'LL NEED IT. PALADIN REECE OUT.

Kira gives me a sideways look as I put the comm-tile back down. "Was that a paladin girlfriend or something?"

"Jealous?"

She takes another bite of her fruit and says, "Maybe. What's up?"

I scoff and put an arm around her and kiss her head. "Just one of my plebes."

She cocks her head in questioning.

"A trainee of sorts. We're assigned a trainee or plebe right after they pass prelims. You know—to show them the ropes, bust their chops, and generally be a pain in their asses. When we think they're ready, they run the Crucible, where we keep them up for three or four days at a time and basically run them through any scenario possible."

"Jeez, sounds awful."

"It is as bad as it sounds, but she's ready. She's a smart and tough kid. She shouldn't have a problem with it. I'm kinda pissed they're running her through it without me. I'm sure it's just another 'fuck you' from Daimyo Corbin."

"How many have you trained?"

I sigh and put my hands on the back of my head, trying to keep a tally. "Well, you don't start training until you're at least five years out of probation, and I think I was about twenty at that point, so I don't know… One a year since then, so maybe fifteen or more."

"Wow. I didn't have anything formal like that. I just left my parents one day. Sink or swim." She nestles into my arms then says, "So who did you have to blow to get two days of leave?"

"Classy, as always."

She shrugs. "That's why you like me."

"True." After eating and taking a few sips of the fluid, I start to feel human again. "Daimyo Raines wants something from me. He's not telling me the whole story—I know it—but there's something brewing. I thought I'd take advantage and ask for a few days of leave. Besides, I've been working my ass off for more than a year without so much as a breather. Thought I deserved it."

"So what they got you on now?" She stops. "Okay, never mind. It's secret. Forget I asked."

I slump down in the pile of pillows and grab her by the waist so she's next to me. "Honestly, I don't even give a shit anymore. The Guild is a fucking joke of what it used to be. When we first met, I was taking down Po because he had stolen vaccines from the Backic Keeper faction. Turns out we didn't retrieve all of the vaccines, and some of them are being sold on the black market."

She's silent for a bit and says, "So they want you to find it?"

"Or whoever is selling it, anyway. I don't think it's one person but probably a few of Po's close associates who knew some of his hiding spots and took it for their own."

"So what happened to Po?"

"You don't want to know."

I lie on my back and ease my head into a mound of pillows. She leans her chest on mine, and I rest a hand on her rump and rub.

"Kira, it's a joke. They have us paladins fighting their stupid little battles all so they can clamor for more votes at the yearly Galactic Council in a few months."

She wrinkles her nose. "I don't get it. I thought all the factions hated each other. How can each of you be bought off by different factions but still operate as a functional group?"

I shrug and take another bite of my fruit. "The Keepers like to put up a front like they are mortal enemies, but really, it's a bunch of rich people with a few minor disagreements. They know it's in their best interest to mostly agree, and they all agree to screw over the little guys."

"Wonderful."

"Yeah, but mark my words: this uneasy equilibrium they have isn't going to last, and it'll tear the Guild to pieces with everyone's alliances. I've pretty well been avoiding that nonsense, but now, Raines is leaning on me hard to run for daimyo."

"You're not actually considering that. Are you?"

"Mostly no. But it would make things a lot easier. I wouldn't have to worry about Corbin and Tabor breathing down my neck constantly."

"You told me Tabor was banned from being a daimyo."

"He was, but if Corbin makes elder and has enough backing, he could easily get that rescinded."

She rolls off my chest to her back. "Argh! This political crap gives me a severe migraine. How in the hell do you deal with it?"

I laugh and roll onto my side and start to draw shapes on her stomach with my fingers. "I don't. I try to spend as much time as possible away from that flippin' planet."

"So you said 'mostly no,' that you weren't going to do the daimyo thing. Is there a chance you will? I mean, don't you have to get married and stuff?"

"Yeah, Raines even showed me my match."

Her jaw clenches, and her eyes burn with hatred.

Oh. Shit. What did I walk into?

She swats my hand off her stomach, and almost in one move, she is away from me. "What do you mean he showed you a match?"

"Kira, hon, I didn't agree to anything. And even if I did, it doesn't mean that we can't still—"

"Oh, it certainly does. I'm not a whore."

I get up from the floor and stand by her. "I know you're not a whore. It's just that they see marriage as a way to seal a deal and make alliances. Just a business deal. Not like us."

"So what are we like, then?"

I sigh and take her hands. "I don't know. I just know that before you, I was ready for my service with the Guild to be over, if you get my meaning. It was all bullshit, and no point in going on. I still think it's all bullshit, but now there is a point in going on." I put her hands to my mouth and graze them over my lips. "I'm not going to do it, Kira. I was just letting you know what happened."

She wraps her arms around my middle and squeezes. "Good."

I take her hand and lead her to our mound of pillows and blankets then wrap both of us up tightly.

She says, "Then don't go back."

I laugh. "What?"

"When your leave is over. Don't go back. Stay with me, and we can be partners. Or wait—that might be too much togetherness. Go make your own collective of mercs. Hell, you just said the Guild's on borrowed time."

I cough on the drink of electrolyte replacement I'm sipping. "Say what? Uh, no. How in the hell do you think I could make that happen?"

Her eyes sparkle, and she smiles. "Seriously, you trained a ton of paladins. Find a few mercs, and give them some real training and direction, then form your own, um… company. I have enough contacts that I could keep you in business for years." Her smile grows as she thinks about the idea more. "Hon, you're too good for the Guild. You can get back to doing what you like and stop dealing with bullshit politics. We could make a hell of a partnership. We could do this."

As tempting as the thought is, I know it could never be. "Kira, hon, they will hunt me down and find me. And since you were an accessory to my escape, they'll put you in a pain amplifier for who knows how long before killing you, just to make an example of you. I can't risk that."

Her eyes are pleading. She swallows a lump in her throat, wipes her eyes, and breathes deeply. "Hannibal, you're smart. You have more choices than you think, but you're too scared to follow a different path than you've always known."

I sigh and hold her tightly. "Let's just enjoy this time we have together, okay?"

She curls into me and breathes out a barely audible, "Okay."

My arms wrap around her, and we nestle under the blankets together, trying to forget the reality surrounding us.

CHAPTER FIFTEEN

THE SUN BEATS DOWN ON me as I cross the abandoned courtyard of the Guild. Daimyo Raines called an immediate meeting with me, and it's been a few months since I've been put on the task of finding the source of the vaccine leak. Since Jordan Burnes was apprehended, the vaccine sales seemed to just disappear. We all know there is someone behind Jordan and all the other sales because Jordan is far too stupid to be the mastermind behind all of this. We also know, according to the vaccines accounted for and what we can see that's been sold, at least five hundred more units should be out there. I, along with some of our best hackers, have been trying to crack the case, and it's ended up in dead end after dead end.

Footsteps echo behind me, and I look over my shoulder. Paladin Cane is running to catch up with me. "Paladin Reece."

"How's it going, Paladin Cane?"

She smiles. "That still sounds weird. Uh, I'm going on my first solo run. Nothing big—just shaking down a few businesses who haven't paid their dues to the Eiker-Pynes faction."

"Good luck, but you don't need it." I continue walking to Raines's office, and she follows.

"Yeah, I know. Hey, you hear anything on the vaccine case yet?"

"Nope. Daimyo Raines wants to meet with me. Maybe he has a break." The office is in sight, and I break away from Cane. "Hey, use your brain and remember your training, and you'll do fine."

"Sir, yes, sir."

I make my way up to Raines's office and check in with his adjutant.

The young man in a stark-white uniform says, "Conference room A. They're all waiting for you."

I scrunch my face. "Who all is waiting for me?"

"I'm not to say anything else. Please proceed to conference room A, Paladin Reece."

My stomach drops and knots. This can't be good. Before opening the door, I take a big breath. Inside, Raines is sitting at the head of the table. To his right is a tiny dark-haired man, and to his left is a statuesque blonde who looks familiar. They all stand when I enter the room.

Raines starts, "Hannibal, good to see you. I want to introduce you to Councilman Rey and his daughter, Helena. He and his daughter are visiting, and I thought while they were here—"

Motherfucker, fuck me. Shit—this is the match. I thought Raines gave up on that.

I don the best smile I can and extend my hand to the woman first. Her blue eyes shimmer, and as I shake her hand, she shows her pearly-white teeth.

"It's very good to meet you, Hannibal," she says. "I was told so much about you."

"All good, I hope."

"Oh, absolutely."

Rey extends his hand, which I take. He says, "Yes, all good. Raines informs us that you have been working our vaccine case very diligently. I was impressed with how you happened on Jordan Burnes. He has yielded some excellent information. How were you able to find him, anyway?"

I clear my throat. "I have a lot of contacts, and they were able to lead me to him. Turns out he's actually a Separatist, and he pissed off…" I look at the woman. "Sorry, ma'am." She waves her hand, passing off the language. I continue, "Anyway, the independent transporters didn't take kindly to him passing himself off as one of their own, so they were pretty quick to sell him out."

Raines laughs. "Two birds with one stone. I told you this was a good one."

The man nods. "Yes, and if what Raines has told me is true, I think we're going to be able to come to a wonderful agreement." He looks at his comm-tile then his daughter. "Come, Helena, we have a few more meetings to attend to here."

She chimes in, "I also have a few holo-cons I need to call into afterward." She looks at me and rolls her eyes. "You would think the CEO you hired would be able to run the businesses you hand to them without checking in with you weekly." She extends her hand again, which I shake. "It was lovely meeting you. I'll comm you later, and we'll have drinks."

"That would be nice, ma'am."

"Helena."

They both leave the room, and I wait for a few seconds to gather my calm. Raines is sitting at the table with a shit-eating grin on his face, and I'm left seething. I sit in the chair.

It takes everything I have to keep from screaming as I ask, "What in the hell was that? I never said I'd enter into a contract with them!"

"You didn't say no."

"Daimyo, sir, I'm just not at a point in my life that I can do this. I really appreciate the offer, but..." I remember Kira's eyes pleading with me. "I just can't."

I start to leave, and he barks at me, "Kira Dresden."

I stand stock-still and turn to look at him. He smiles and motions to me to sit, and I do.

"I'm not stupid, Hannibal. I know exactly why you took leave a few months ago. I also know who your 'contact' is. It's okay. We all have a little side action going on here and there. I'm not going to fault you there. She is a looker."

I claw my fingers into my leg to keep myself from punching him in the face. Through my clenched jaw, I say, "So what's your point? She was integral in finding Burnes."

"Just that you seem to be getting in a little deep with her." He waves his hand. "Or maybe not. I don't know—don't really give a shit, either. What I do know and what I do give a shit about is Corbin. He's gaining favor with the elders. I need more daimyos in my court. I have a match made for you. I have the pledge of at least six daimyos that will vouch for you. It's yours. All you have to do is sign the contract."

I narrow my eyes. "Or?"

"Or I will no longer protect you as a paladin as I have since you came back from the Po run. You're on your own, and how long do you think you'll last? And what of your contact, lover, whatever... Kira? How long do you think she'll last with Tabor on the prowl? From what I hear, he has a bone to pick with her."

A fire rages in my body. I'm paralyzed by anger and fear. For the first time in my life, I have no idea what to do.

Raines smiles and says, "I've sent the contract to your comm-tile. There's only two things you have to do. Sign the contract."

I sigh, and my body feels like it's going to cave in on itself. "And?"

"We have strong intel about where the vaccine is coming from. Find it and bring us the perp. The conference is happening next month, and the Backics are starting to get more than edgy to get their votes. Once you deliver the vaccines and they get their votes, Rey and his daughter will agree to the contract. It's so easy a plebe could do it."

I don't have a choice. My hand has been forced. I get up from the table and walk toward the door. I mumble, "Fine. I'll get your vaccine and sign your damn contract. Leave Kira out of it. She's done nothing to the Guild."

"You've made a great choice. We'll have all the information ready for you in a few days. I expect you to have all your provisions ready and your plans made within a week."

I walk out the door without another word.

CHAPTER SIXTEEN

MY ROOM IS DARK AND cold, and I slink into my chair and throw back another glass of scotch. I've lost count of how many I've had. I've spent the last hour going back and forth from the marriage contract to pictures of Kira. Getting involved with her was stupid, anyway. I got burned, and I knew it would happen. Throughout the night, I try to convince myself she never meant that much to me, anyway, that she knew it was all in fun. But I know better. For a few seconds, I consider never contacting her again, just cutting ties cold turkey. But she deserves more than that. She saved my life on more than one occasion and in more than one way. For a moment, I knew what it was like to truly care for someone else, and I think that's what the Guild was afraid of the most. No, I owe her more than that. I make a few swipes to my comm-tile, and it rings. With every unanswered ring, my stomach knots and churns, and I pace.

There she is, bleary-eyed, with her beautiful eyes shining and hair a tangled mess. "I synced our tiles so you wouldn't call me when I was in sleep cycle, numb nuts. I hope this isn't a late-night booty call holo style because I'm not in the mood. What do you want?"

My words are slow to come. "I, uh, made daimyo."

The look on her face is hard to discern, but she certainly looks alert and awake now. She brushes the hair out her face and scowls at me. "So you woke me up to tell me to fuck off, then. Right?"

"No, Kira, it doesn't have to be that way."

She glares at me with hate in her eyes. I can't take it, so I look away.

"I told you—I'm not a whore. You fucking chose, you piece of shit! You've always chosen that life over me. They don't care about you like—" She's silent for a bit. "Never fuckin' mind."

"Kira, you don't understand. It has to be this way. I tried. I tried."

She shakes her head. "You ruined everything. Now I have to deal with *this* by myself."

"Deal with what?"

She shakes her head silently, tears streaming.

"What the hell are you talking about? What do you have to deal with?"

"Fuck you. It doesn't even matter now. You have important daimyo things to do. Go suck an elder's dick, because you'll be doing that a lot now."

My chest feels like it's going to cave in. "Kira, I—" I stop myself midsentence. We knew what we were getting into before we started this thing. I direct all my rage at her. "You know what, fuck you too! Don't pretend like this was anything more than profit for you and a little fun when you got bored. You said you weren't a whore, but we all know that you were fucking me for a profit." As the words leave my mouth, I feel ashamed and broken. I feel tears stream from my good eye.

She screams at the screen, "You know what? No one will ever love you because you're a piece of shit who's only out for himself. Don't ever try to get in contact with me again."

The screen goes black. I throw my glass into the wall and scream. It's over now, but she's safe.

I spend the next several days in a drunken stupor and trying to commit to memory as much of the intel as I can. I still feel a gaping wound in my heart that feels like it will never heal, and perhaps it never will. I would give anything never to feel this way again. It was my own fault—I played with fire I should never have touched. The incessant glaring of the sun makes my head ache and pound more than it already does. As I heave the last of my equipment onto my ship, my stomach gurgles and churns, not only because of the late-night benders, but also because of what awaits me in the future. I sold my soul, and there's nothing that can be done about it now. I look at my comm-tile to check the route to the vaccines. It looks like it's in the remote Vela system, at least a two-week trip. Good—at least a couple-week stay of execution from my new life.

The sound of a throat clearing makes me look up. It's Cane.

I breathe deeply, and not taking an eye off my tile, I say, "What is it?"

She stammers nervously, "Uh, sir, I just want to talk to you about my upcoming run."

I grumble, "You don't have to call me sir any longer. We're the same rank."

"From what I heard, that won't be much longer. Thought I'd keep it up, since you'll be a daimyo soon."

No one in this damn place can keep their noses in their own business. I look away from my comm-tile at the smiling blonde and give her a stare that communicates how bad I am feeling. Her smile turns down.

"What do you want?"

"Like I said, I have this run, and—"

The sound of her voice pierces through my skull. I rub my forehead and look at her. "Cane. You're a paladin now, and I have shit to get done. Grow the fuck up and figure out your own run."

Her eyes narrow, and her body stiffens. "Will do, *Paladin* Reece."

She turns and walks away without another word.

My shoulders slump, and I immediately feel bad for what I said. *Ah, fuck it. Kid's got to grow a thick skin, being in the Guild. Besides, I'll apologize when I get back.* I jump in my ship and make a few last checks.

"Paladin Reece to flight control: permission to take off?"

I hear static then "Paladin Reece, you are a go."

I push back on the throttle, and in a blink, the skies turn from a bright blue to a satin black dotted with stars. I punch in the coordinates given to me and slouch back in my seat and wait for my inevitable fate.

CHAPTER SEVENTEEN

THE TRIP TO THE VELA system was a quiet one that gave me the opportunity to catch up on sleep and hydration. Throughout the trip, I considered sending Kira a message to explain everything, but I thought better of it. It's best we leave these things in the past. It's time to grow up and face what I have ahead of me. The feelings of doubt and remorse still fill me, but I've put them aside. I know they will always be there and leave a scar, but I can do nothing about it now. It's time to get on with another stage of my life. The die is cast, and I need to live with the repercussions of my decisions.

A new message appears on my comm-tile:

> I WILL BE VISITING THE GUILD NEXT WEEK WITHOUT MY FATHER. WE NEED TO SCHEDULE DRINKS AND GET TO KNOW EACH OTHER BETTER.

I sigh. *No use prolonging it.* This is my fate. It could be a lot worse. I respond:

> **I SHOULD BE BACK BY THEN. MY CALENDAR IS PUBLIC. HAVE YOUR ASSISTANT PICK A CONVENIENT TIME FOR YOU.**

> I WAS THINKING MAYBE A NIGHTTIME DATE. WHO KNOWS WHERE THAT WILL LEAD.

> **UNTIL THEN...**

The comm-tile goes dark, and I give another sigh then pull up the intel Raines gave me. I have a course to a minor planet preloaded by the Guild's nav experts. For a second, I think of pulling up the "good" star charts Kira loaded on here and recharting the course, but I stop myself. I need to get those off of here, anyway. I'm sure they don't meet regs. All that seems like a lifetime ago now.

I shake those thoughts and look at the intel. Apparently, the planet I'm headed to is an old mining planet abandoned years ago. A plethora of caves and shafts are there, which would make a great hiding spot for any contraband. The person or persons pulling this off was very skilled at hiding their signature. The vaccine was always sold to different planets and never in huge quantities at one time. No specific vendor ever came up at the end of their searches, and any lead our cyber experts got would end up in dead end after dead end. Then someone got the clever idea to stop using cyber to track the perp but to use triangulation of the shipment destinations. They came up with a few planets that were central to all the destinations. Since this planet, which has long since lost its name, was a former mining colony with shafts and caves, it was the prime suspect for harboring our goods and, I hoped, the perp. I rub my temples. I just want all of this to be over with as soon as possible so I can get on with the rest of my miserable fucking life.

A star chart pops up on my display, indicating I'm within an hour of the planet. I start scans on all comm-tile wavelengths to ascertain if anyone is there. If no one is home, that'll make getting the goods that much easier. Then I just need to wait for whoever to come for their items, then I swoop in and make the grab. Yep, so easy a plebe could do it. I lie back in my seat and listen to the spectrum analyzer sift through the waves for some kind of hit. Then I hear it, a squall and a squeal indicating traffic.

"All right, you fucker, let's see what you got for me," I mutter.

After a few clicks to my console, text is displayed in front of me.

REQUESTING 20 UNITS FOR—

STOP THERE. DON'T TELL ME WHO YOU ARE. DO YOU HAVE ANYTHING I ASKED FOR IN MY BARTER REQUEST?

YES, SIR. A GROSS OF RATION BARS, 500 POUNDS OF WATER PURIFIER, PRENATAL VITAMINS, SEEDS, HYDROPONIC SUPPLIES, FIRST-AID SUPPLIES, AND 10 UNITS OF ANTIBIOTIC.

Prenatal vitamins? This asshole is smart—dealing in credits is way too easy to track. Bartering for goods then selling those goods on other planets in exchange for credits—brilliant. I'm sure that communiqué was bounced all over the galaxy before it got here too. I was just lucky to be close enough to the source to catch it.

THAT IS ACCEPTABLE. I WILL SEND YOU INSTRUCTIONS LATER ON WHERE TO DROP THE ITEMS.

A half smile comes to my face. Looks like someone is home and my job will be over sooner than I thought.

As I head for the planet, I narrow down the source of the communiqué to a few square miles. Raines was right—they handed this one right to me. There has to be a catch.

When the shuttle lands, I check the outside atmospherics. The wind is a steady gust, and the temperature is a balmy negative ten. I grab my wool-lined leather coat and a few armaments.

"I guess it's now or never, Reece."

Once I'm outside the ship on the planet, visibility goes to next to nothing, with snow and debris blowing around. My synthetic eye can make out IR signatures, and in the distance, I see a faint but glowing signature. I look at my comm-tile and overlay maps of this planet and see a cave about two klicks ahead. The wind and debris pelt me as I make my way toward the cave. Within a half klick of the cave, I survey it again with my augmented eye. This time, I can make out a medium freighter and one person. I ready my weapon and close in on the entrance of the cave, and I'm met with a volley of fire. I see a boulder and leap behind it, exchanging fire with my assailant.

A voice echoes through the cave. "Get on out of here. There's nothing you're looking for here."

I fire a few more shots and am met with a few in return.

The voice rings out again. "Just be on your way. I don't want any trouble."

That voice. My body runs cold, and my heart skips.

Oh no… No, it can't be.

I have to force enough breath out of my mouth to say, "Kira!"

CHAPTER EIGHTEEN

I SLOWLY RISE FROM THE BOULDER I'm hiding behind and walk into the cave. "Kira! Is that you?" I hear silence and don't see her with either eye. "Kira, let's talk."

I walk farther into the cave. Lights are on throughout, but it is still dark and shadowed. Kira's little Goddard-class freighter sits in the middle of the mammoth opening. My breath speeds as I walk into the darkness.

"Kira, was that you? We can work this out."

"Doubt it!"

A crushing pain sears through my arm. I turn around, and she is standing above me on a ledge of the cave. Another searing pain grazes my cheek this time.

"Damn it! Let's talk this out."

"Talk what out? You came here to kill me, and I know a paladin never misses their mark. Was killing me a condition of getting your fucking rank?"

Another shot is fired but this time misses me.

"No, I mean yes, but I didn't know it was you."

The truth of it all is suddenly clear: Raines knew Kira was behind all this. He sent me out here to kill the very last shred of my humanity. I look up at her on the ledge with her gun trained on me. My heart breaks all over again. He never meant her to be safe, ever. I drop my gun and slump to the ground. I lift my hands.

"I'm done, Kira. I'm not going to kill you."

"Seriously?"

I kick my gun away from me then reach into my jacket and throw the rest of my arms to the ground away from me. "I'm done. I'm done with it all. If you need to take me out, then do it. I'd rather it be at your hands than anyone else's. But even if I don't get you, someone else will eventually. They're not giving up on this one."

I hear footsteps coming closer to me, then she's in view.

She slumps next to me, in tears. "I fucked up."

"That would qualify for the understatement of the year. What in the fuck are you doing with all this?"

She shrugs. "When you planted that worm and gave me Po's commtile, I saw he had the vaccine. Thought if I was smart about it and not too greedy, I could live on it for a bit. So do you have to kill me now?"

"In theory. But I told you I ain't doing it. The only reason I agreed to be a daimyo was so they'd leave you alone. But now, Kira, you're in some deep shit. I would run to the ends of the galaxy with you, but they'll find us."

She sobs. I wrinkle my eyebrows. *This is not like her.*

"I just need some time. Just a little time. How long do you think we can evade them?"

The pain in my arms is starting to take over. I can't think clearly. *What in the hell is wrong with her?* I clench my jaw and breathe out my nose. "Kira, why do you need time? Is it to complete that transaction? I'm sorry to say that ship has sailed. I'd say even if we scrubbed our identities and hopped all over the galaxy, we're basically limited to the supplies we have, and I have maybe a week's worth. Once we have to stop to get supplies or get refueled, we're done."

She puts her head between her knees, and her body shakes. I rub her back.

"If only I could've gotten that last transaction, that would've held me through," she says. "Damn it! I don't have any provisions. That transaction was supposed to be it. I knew I needed to get off grid for a while, and you breaking it off with me made my decision easier." She leans her head back and rubs her face. "Blast it, Reece. This is your problem too. You have to help me figure this out."

I wince at the pain raging through my body. *I can't believe she's blaming me for this.*

"I didn't do anything. You're the one who stole the vaccine. I mean,

I actually applaud the ballsy move, but you knew the danger of stealing from the Keepers."

She closes her eyes and breathes out, "Oh my God, you are stupid. I'm not talking about that. You have responsibilities, Hannibal. I should've told you sooner, but I wasn't sure until right before you called me. I didn't think that was a good time to say anything, so I didn't. I thought I could deal with this by myself. I can't. I need help."

My frustration levels are going through the roof. I wish this woman would stop being so fucking cryptic. "Kira, hon, my arm and face are killing me. Is there any way you can be less—"

Then our past conversation echoes back to me: *"I have to deal with this by myself."* Also, her provisions included prenatal vitamins.

My. God. "Kira, are you—"

I don't need an answer. It's in her tear-strewn face. I take her in my arms, and we hold each other and cry.

CHAPTER NINETEEN

M Y PAIN SUBSIDES AS KIRA puts the last seam of glue in to close my wounds. She walks away in silence to put away the medical equipment, leaving me staring at the ceiling. My mind is racing with everything that has been thrown at me in the last few hours. I look at Kira, who is washing her hands, and think of everything she is going through now. The usually self-assured woman looks scared and hopeless. Sure, what she did was stupid and risky, but that's a hazard of her occupation. If you want to stay one step ahead of the competition, you have to take risks. This was just one she miscalculated. Add to the mix the fact that she's... No—*we* are now responsible for another life.

"Kira."

She barely gives me a glance and turns back to cleaning and putting away her medical equipment.

"Kira, come here and talk to me."

She barely squeaks out, "Can't. I have to clean this."

"Fuck that. It'll be there when we're done talking. Just c'mere."

She shuffles over to me and sits on the ground, facing me. She leans forward and brushes her hand along my chin and smiles. "I never noticed you had a red birthmark here before."

"I think I had more of a beard every time I saw you." I rub her legs, and for a moment, we stare at each other, saying nothing. "I'm sorry I made it hard for you to tell me."

Tears stream down her face. "I'm not getting rid of it. Although that might be a moot point now."

I stiffen and ask, "Did I ask you to?"

She wipes her tears with the back of her hand. "I guess I could just feel it coming. God, Hannibal, we're so stupid, but you know I wouldn't change anything I did. Well, okay. Maybe in hindsight, stealing the vaccine was ill-advised." When I laugh, she cracks a little smile. "But between us, I wouldn't change a thing. It's weird—I've just always felt at home with you. I can't explain it. I'm not going to say anything sappy like it was love at first sight, because honestly, I was just looking to have fun, and you seemed like you were up for a good time. But it's always been—"

I finish her sentence: "Comfortable, fun, nice…"

She takes my hand in hers. "Exactly. I don't really have much of that in my life."

"Me, neither. I have no one in my life except you. When you asked me to stay when I was on leave, I should've done it, but I was scared."

She shrugs. "I'm not surprised, given the way you were raised."

Finally confronting the elephant in the room, I ask, "What was your plan, anyway? I mean you said you don't want to get rid of it, and you had all those provisions. Were you going to float out in the middle of space and raise our kid as some deep-space hermit, selling hydroponic goods at various stops, hoping you didn't get caught?"

She laughs and wipes the tears from her eyes then swats me. "Our. Kid. That sounds weird."

I nod in agreement.

"But no, I had a plan. Have I ever told you about my cousin Mark?" When I shake my head, she continues, "My family was always the black sheep of the extended family, but me and Mark always hit it off. We've kept up over the years. He and my parents… and you are the only constants in my life." She takes a deep breath. "He and his spouse, Ian, have been looking to adopt, but verifying that you're not buying from a sicko baby farm is costly and difficult. So I was going to float until I had the kid and give it to him. I have it all worked out with him and Ian. They're great men. Super nerdy, boring, engineers. They could give her a life I could never give her, even if I wasn't on the lam. I figured whatever happened to me after that was my own doing." She puts a hand to her belly. "She doesn't deserve to pay for my stupidity."

"She? How can you tell?"

"Um, when I couldn't deny it any longer, I went to those medibot express scanners at the first way station I could get to. The scan said it was a girl and that I'm due in, uh…" She looks at her comm-tile. "Like a little over five months now."

I motion for her to come sit next to me. I need her close to me. I slowly lift an arm so that she can nestle into me.

Before she does, she sits up straight to face me and says, "I'm even starting to get fat now. Wanna feel, or is that too weird?"

"No, not at all."

I put a hand on her belly. What used to be soft and giving now has a bit of firmness behind it. I trace my fingers along her smooth skin and small, perfectly round lump. Our child. I lean in and feather a light kiss on Kira's lips and breathe out, "I'm sorry, I should've been there for you."

She leans into me gently, avoiding my wound. "Ah, Hannibal, there's no way you could've known. For the first couple of months, I was in denial. I thought it might be stress or I miscalculated or just whatever stupid excuse I could think of. Then, when there was no further denying it and the medibot thing gave me her vitals and a picture…" She swipes her comm-tile and shows me a picture of something that resembles a tadpole.

I screw up my face and say, "Hope she doesn't look that weird when she comes out."

She slaps me and says, "Shut up, stupid. She's supposed to look like that now. Well, after that, I stopped drinking."

"Holy shit!"

"I know, right! Honestly, I thought about getting lost after you told me that you got Jordan Burnes for distributing vaccine." She rolls her eyes and sighs and hesitantly says, "But I guess I didn't want to leave you." She squeezes my hand and says quickly, as if trying to absolve herself from any sin, "And by the way, if I had known that Jordan Burnes was at the other end of that transaction, I never would've sold it to him, because he's a fucking dumbass fool. I need to figure out how I can work that angle better."

I take a deep breath and say, "Kira, hon, I didn't mean anything I said."

"I know. Me neither." She sighs. "But now, I have no idea what to do. We obviously can't hide out here forever or at least until I can get the baby to safety."

I growl and shake my head. "It's all bullshit. The only reason we're here is because the Backic Keeper faction is clamoring for a few extra votes at the Galactic Conference. They don't want to be behind the Independent Council of Planets for votes, so they're trading vaccines for votes with other factions who have a higher number of votes. It's insanity, and now the Guild is all wrapped up in it. It wasn't always that way. We were truly independent. If a small band of colonials collected enough money, then we'd help. Now, we exclusively do business with the Keepers. It's all about power and politics."

She gets a look on her face I know well.

"What are you thinking, Kira?"

"What if we could kind of help the little people out and maybe save our asses?"

"What are you thinking?"

"The Independent Council contacted me about getting a large shipment of vaccine for the hardest hit planets. I refused because it would put a big frickin' target on my head. Guess it's too late to avoid that."

I get a big smile on my face, lean in, and give her a big kiss on the cheek. "You're a genius. I know the Backic faction doesn't care who the votes come from. A vote's a vote. Honestly, I think they never thought of it because no one ever gives the Independent Council a second thought."

"I know. I'm always saving your ass. I'm pretty sure the Independent Council is hurting enough for vaccine at this point they'll give whatever votes the Backics want."

I get up and extend a hand to her, and she follows. I look at my comm-tile to ascertain how long I've been out of communication with the Guild. They're going to start getting suspicious soon. "Okay, look, I'll get in contact with the Backics and work out a deal. You get in contact with the Independent Council and work your end. Before that, I need to get in contact with the Guild. I've been out of contact with them long enough it's going to set off red flags."

As if on cue, a bang comes at the door of the ship, and someone calls out, "I'm looking for Kira Dresden!"

I hang my head. "Son of a bitch."

CHAPTER TWENTY

"**O**NE OF YOUR FRIENDS?"

The person calls out again, "Kira Dresden! Come out peacefully."

I heave a big sigh. "Let me take care of this. I might be able to talk my way out of it."

She tucks a gun into the back of my pants. "In case you're not able to talk your way out of it."

I go to the rear of the ship and press a few buttons, and the cargo bay starts down slowly. As the ramp whines and creaks, I yell, "Don't shoot! It's Paladin Reece. I have this situation under control."

The cargo ramp is fully extended, and I start down with my hands up. No one is in sight. Generally, a paladin makes runs on their own unless they are training a plebe. Nobody had a reason to send a whole team. As far as they know, it's just Kira and me here.

I yell again, "The situation is under control!"

Then Paladin Cane appears from behind a rock formation, her gun trained on me.

Shit damn fuck.

"Paladin Reece, are you okay? I saw blood on the ground."

"I'm fine. Go back to the Guild and tell them I have this in hand. Why did they send you, anyway? This was an easy job—no need for backup."

She narrows her eyes and fixates on my chest and patched-up arm and face. I probably should've put my shirt back on.

"Why are you shirtless, Paladin Reece? Where is the perp?"

I say slowly and softly, "Listen, Cane, just get back in your ship and go back to the Guild and tell them I have this in hand. It's going to be okay."

"No, it's not. Where is she? That's the girl you were going to see a few months back, wasn't it?"

I'm silent, just staring her down, wondering what bullshit they filled her mind with.

"They were right about you. You're not for the Guild. Hell, the way you talked about the Guild being owned by the Keepers and your flagrant disrespect for the daimyos, and now this… taking up with that whore!"

"Watch yourself, Cane! You don't know the whole story. You're being played. Just go back to your ship and get out of here."

I detect a bit of a tremble and hope I can play up her fear of me.

She shakes her head and stares me down. "I'm for the Guild, Reece. I'm going to take you in, get the shipment, and kill the bitch."

I shake my head. "I can't let you do that." Without thinking, in one motion, I reach for my gun and pull the trigger. Cane crumples in a pile on the ground. I clench my jaw and head back to the ship.

Kira is waiting for me at the top of the ramp. "You know her?"

As I pass Kira, I say somberly, "She was the last plebe I trained. I know they sent her here because they thought I'd be easy on her. They were playing with me. I hate every one of them for making me do that."

Kira presses a button on the wall of the ship and puts her arms around me and whispers, "I'm sorry."

"It's okay. You two are my family now."

She gives a sad smile.

I head to the cockpit and say, "C'mon, we don't have long. Let's get all the provisions we can off my ship and get out of here then make some deals."

I walk into the cockpit of the ship from the cargo bay after being online with the Backic faction. Kira has her feet kicked up on the console of her ship, swaying to tunes playing in the background. I crane my head around the captain's seat and land a peck on Kira's cheek then sit in the copilot seat next to her.

She turns down the music. "What did they say?"

"They're game. I could see they were surprised they didn't think of it."

"What are the terms?"

"They want no fewer than three of the Independent Council's voting seats for two years. In return, the Independent Council will get the remainder of the vaccine and consideration for the next batch of vaccine not spoken for at cost plus five percent."

"Hmm, not a bad negotiation. Now the important part: what about us?"

"I'm glad you asked. If we secure the seats at the agreed-on terms before the council meeting next week, then we are under their protection. They are going to call off all hits on us, starting now. However, they aren't going to extend their full protection until we complete the job. Which means the Guild is damn sure going to send people after us to intercept our deal just so we don't make a fool of them and because they hate me."

"Do we get any assistance?"

"Just free use of their holes. The way they see it is that they wouldn't give the Guild help to complete the job, so why should they give us help?"

Kira clucks her tongue. "I could've negotiated better."

"Doubt it. Ms. Rey has a crush on me."

Kira gives me a stink eye that chills me to my core.

"Kidding. Jeez. So you gonna give your contact a call?"

She leans over the console and pushes a few buttons, and text is displayed:

CONNECTING PLEASE HOLD.

She looks over at me as we wait. "Ever do it with a pregnant lady?"

Right before she finishes her question, a dowdy-looking brunette is displayed on the vidscreen. "What did you say? Who is this, and how did you get this signature?"

Kira sits bolt upright, and I nearly have to bite my tongue to contain my laughter.

Kira narrows her eyes at me then looks at the vidscreen. "Sorry, ma'am. My name is Kira Dresden, independent transporter. I was made aware of your need for the Ethos virus vaccine, and I think I might have a line on a deal that might be very beneficial to you and yours."

The woman scowls at Kira. "How did you get these signatures?"

"Remember last month when you wanted a hundred fifty units and were denied?"

The woman's eyes go wide.

"Yeah, that was me. I assume you got the fifty I was able to deliver and it worked?"

"Yes, we did, and it saved many lives. I will gladly take anything you can provide."

"What about four hundred units?"

My eyes narrow at her. I know she has at least five hundred units. This is no time for her to be playing another con. She ignores me and continues with the exchange.

The woman on the screen stutters, "I… I don't know if we have the capital for that."

"Well, I think it's time we get more creative than just credits or bartering. Are you willing to keep an open mind?"

"It depends."

"Good answer." Kira waves for me to come over. "I have a representative from the Backic faction here, who is willing to offer you four hundred units in exchange for five of your voting seats for three years and consideration for the next batch of vaccine not spoken for at cost plus ten percent."

The woman is silent for a moment while she types on her comm-tile. Then she says, "I'm in communication with the rest of our council. This is going to take a minute."

"Fine. My associate and I can wait." Kira looks up at me and whispers, "You didn't answer my question."

Before I have a chance to answer, the woman comes back on. "Five seats is far too many. We need a voice at the council. We cannot give that up."

Kira looks like she's thinking then says, "One second. Me and my associate have to talk in private." She blacks out the screen and turns to me. "Seriously, have you ever done it with a pregnant lady?"

I smile and kiss her. "No. Maybe I can find out what that's like shortly."

"If you're lucky." She turns the screen back on and looks exasperated. "Look, ma'am, I'm cutting into my negotiating fees for this, but I see all the suffering going on here, and I'm willing to help you out. If you give them four seats for two years, they'll give you..." She looks up at me, and I nod. "Okay, um, four hundred fifty units and consideration on a new batch at cost plus seven percent. Seriously, ma'am, I had to give up my inventory to make this happen."

"One minute, please." After a few seconds, she's back on the screen and nods vigorously. "It's a deal. We will meet and sign on terms and get the vaccine two days before the Galactic Council meeting. If you're not there by then, our deal is null and void."

"Yes, ma'am. Good doing business with you."

The screen goes dark, and Kira turns to me, grinning from ear to ear. "That, my friend, is how you make a deal."

I growl at her, "That still leaves fifty units unaccounted for."

"Hey, you never know if we'll need to use those to barter with. If not, we just 'find' them in our inventory when we get there and throw them in for free."

CHAPTER TWENTY-ONE

A STAR CHART FLOATS IN FRONT of us on the bridge of the ship. Kira studies the chart intently, flipping it this way and that. Periodically, she makes calculations on her comm-tile then looks back at the star chart. She looks over at me. "You said only Backic holes, right?"

I nod. "Yeah, I'll bet you a beer—"

She growls.

"Sorry. I'll pay you in full after you have the little nugget, but anyways… Sure as anything, the Guild has asked other Keeper factions to report if we use their holes. They have all their eyes and ears open for us now. That's why I told you to turn off any device that would transmit information about the ship."

"I was going to do that anyway."

She looks back up at the charts and continues studying and manipulating, biting her lip then pacing. "Damn, I gotta tell ya. It's going to be tight, even taking advantage of all the temporal fluff. Look here—" She blows up the charts so that I can see the different wormholes mapped out with their relative location to the delivery point. "Backic's holes are pretty close to where we are now, but they don't really end up close to our destination. So we're going to have to either haul ass through some shifty disputed territory or venture through some Eiker-Pynes territory. The Eiker-Pynes way is shorter, but—"

I finish her sentence, "A greater chance of getting caught."

"Yeah, but the disputed territory isn't that much longer, but sure as hell, there will be some pirates giving us shit, which will cause loss of time. Plus, if I were the Guild, I'd put people out here no matter what. Then again, y'all aren't that great at mapping routes, either."

I nod in agreement. For all the experts we have making nav charts for us, they can't top Kira's skill at charting routes. I think it's part survival, part hands-on skill, and she's just got a sixth sense about navigation.

We're both silent for a while, pondering our options. Then I say, "We can go into a spiral of self-doubt on this one. You did hold fifty units of vaccine back. We'll use that as barter if we get detained by any unsavory individuals. And we'll take our chances on meeting any paladins either way. Seems to me the shorter route has a greater chance of getting caught, and we won't be able to negotiate our way out of anything there."

She smiles. "Spoken like a true independent transporter. You're really starting to get the hang of this lifestyle." She clicks her console and says, "I'm setting a course. We should be there in three days, fourteen minutes, and thirteen seconds. This gives us about a day of fluff time."

I take a deep breath. "Let's do it."

After traversing the wormhole, we started sleeping in shifts, not really trusting the proximity sensors to alert us if anyone got close. We spent the last day on pins and needles, waiting for something to come along and put all our careful planning in the shitter. In my opinion, it's not really a matter of *if* it'll happen but *when*… and being ready for it when it does.

An alarm echoes through our quarters, and I sit upright, throw off the covers, and rush to the cockpit. In the cockpit, Kira is calmly pushing a few levers and typing something into the console. She works as if the ship is just part of her, not questioning her moves, just doing. I've always had a great respect for what Kira does. She's a one person crew who negotiates, fixes anything that needs fixed, fights off pirates or general assholes, navigates, and anything else that assures her survival. Seeing her work firsthand gives me an all-new appreciation of her. As if sensing my presence, she looks over her shoulder and smiles.

"Sorry. Did the alarm wake you?"

"Yeah. I wasn't really sleeping great, anyway. What's up?"

"Nothing new. The inertial dampeners need to be replaced soon. The manufacturer always tells you to replace them every two thousand hours, but you can get a good three thousand out of them before they need to be replaced. It's their way of getting you to buy more shit than you need."

"How many hours do these have on them?"

She waves a hand. "Eh, like twenty-eight hundred or something."

My eyes go wide.

"It'll be fine. Three thousand's conservative."

"If you say so." I change the subject. "So what's next?"

"What do you mean?"

"We deliver the vaccine. All of our sins are forgiven, except by the Guild, but fuck them. What do we do?"

"Oh, you mean like us and, um, this one," she says, pointing at her belly.

"Yeah…"

"I've been thinking about it a lot while you sleep back there. I've never been one to take the easy way out, which is why I deliberated about it a lot, and obviously I need your input, too, but—" She starts to tear up. "Hannibal, I'm glad you're with me now, and I trust you'll never go back to the Guild, but I don't think it changes my decision about what to ultimately do about this little one. I know I told you my childhood was pretty good, but there were also some pretty terrible moments too. Mom and Dad are great, but Mom and Dad are more about themselves than they ever were about me. There were times we had to make five ration bars last three weeks. When I was five, I had to hang out in orbit by myself for a week because Mom had to rescue Dad from a deal that went bad. They loved me—I know that—but I went through some shit no kid should have to, and look at us. We're no different."

I squeeze her hand.

"Honestly, I don't want to change, and I think if I tried and you tried, it would last for just a little while, and we'd end up hating each other."

As much as I want to disagree with her, to say that we could make it work, that we could keep the little one safe… The logical part of my brain knows it's not true. People are always going to be gunning for us and for the kid, to get to us. As soon as that thought comes, my stomach sinks.

"Kira, you're right, and it's not the easy thing to do. It's easy to think we'll be able to make it work, but we'd just end up screwing up the kid. There's something important, though. We can't have this easy-peasy, see-her-on-occasion type of relationship. We have to minimize the number of people who know we have a kid."

She narrows her eyes. "Why? You afraid you're going to lose your tough-guy card?"

"No. Listen, no one has ever left the Guild alive. Hopefully, all this ends up with me as the first one, but sure as hell, they're going to think I have some kind of debt to pay since I was sold into servitude to them. What better way to get even than—"

Her face goes slack. "I… I didn't even think about that." She starts to cry and says through the tears, "I just want to do someone some good in this galaxy. This is probably my only chance."

I wipe away her tears and give her a long, lingering kiss. "You already did, hon. I think we're doing the right thing."

As if to distract us from the heartbreak that awaits us, the proximity sensor sounds.

I look at Kira. "Is that sensor working?"

"Afraid so. Hirabah raiding party hailing us now."

CHAPTER TWENTY-TWO

THE SOUNDS OF THE ALARM fill the cabin. Kira calmly silences them and pulls up an image on the vidscreen.

Inside the cockpit, a grainy image of a man in dark-brown dreadlocks and jade eyes smiles at the camera. "Are you lost, friends?"

Kira gives a charming smile and says, "Hello, friend. Name's Lara Jean, and this here's the hubs, Rusty. We're just a couple of independent transporters on our way to Talus-9 for that, uh… What you call it, hon?"

I say in monotone, "Galactic Conference."

"Oh, yeah, that's right. Anyways, we're gonna try to sell some shit to the richies who go to that shindig. No big deal."

The man on the video screen responds, "What kind of shit are you trying to sell? Maybe we'll be interested in buying it. It's still a long way off. Save you a trip."

Kira mutes the comms. "He doesn't want to buy shit. He wants to take it."

I mumble, "Duh. How are you going to talk your way out of this one, slick?"

"I got this." She unmutes the comms. "Ah, you probably won't be interested in what we got—shit the richies like: fish eggs and snails. Disgusting, if you ask me, but ya know, to each his own." She types a message in her comm-tile to me while talking to the man. "I remember this one time a dude asked me to bring him horse testicles. Can you believe that shit?"

A message pops up on my tile:

> MAN THE WEAPONS SYSTEM. IT'S THE PART OF
> THE CONSOLE OUTLINED IN RED. I'M SURE YOU
> CAN FIGURE THE REST OF IT OUT.

I give her a slight nod and slink over to the copilot seat.

In the background, she keeps yammering, "Then this one lady… She wanted 'back massagers.' Well, you know what that means. She's, like, all uppity and shit, and I'm like, 'Girl, it's good. We all have needs, and—'"

The man on the screen growls, "That's enough." He breathes in and regains his composure. "Now, friend, it's customary that when passing through our turf, you give us some kind of symbol of goodwill to pass through… unscathed."

She dons a surprised look. "Oh my. I had no idea. I didn't bring enough for you fellas. Tell y'all what—when we get back from selling stuff at the richie planet, I'll bring ya back something real nice. What do you want?"

The man is silent, looking at Kira in disbelief, then bellows, "I'm tired of playing nice! I want your shit. Give it to us or prepare to be boarded."

"Fuck. Off."

At that, she turns off the vidscreen, and I introduce a few shots into the belly of their raider. She hits the throttle and speeds past the gigantic ship. I look at the console, and the alarms and lights are going wild. I quickly silence them.

"They are right on our tail, Kira. We can't keep up this pace."

"No shit. You got any better ideas? My shit self-defense isn't a match for their arsenal. I'm not willing to barter with the vaccine yet because if we offer a bit, they'll take it all," she says, gaze intent on the skies in front of her.

"My thinking exactly."

The ship shimmies and sways as Kira taxes the system to its max. I close my eyes and mentally run through everything I brought on board from my ship, then I remember one item in my inventory that should do the trick. "I have an idea, but you're going to have to slow down for it to work."

She purses her lips, and not taking her eyes away from the scene in front of her, she says, "Fine, I trust you. Just make it work, and let me know when to slow down."

"Yes, ma'am."

I'm out of the cockpit and in our quarters in seconds. I say a prayer under my breath that I brought the item. Then I see the bulky black plastic box. I unlock it, and inside are a few ion-pulse drones and some associated explosives. I run through the power up and sync sequence, which seems to be taking painfully long. One by one, all the drones glow green.

I yell to the cockpit, "How you doin', hon?"

"Never been better. If you're going to do something, do it fast."

"On it." I go to the rear of the ship then yell, "Engage environmental shields!"

"Shields engaged."

I type in the code for the ramp, and it lowers. As soon as the opening is big enough, I ready the drones and yell, "Slow it down, babe!"

The ship slows, and the raiders come into view and send a volley of fire. Our ship bucks and sways. I focus on my comm-tile and plug in a few commands, and the drones rise and fly out of the cargo hold through the environmental shield. My comm-tile displays real-time images from the drones. I hope they are too small to be detected by their radar. Our ship bucks again under another volley of fire.

Kira yells, "Hurry up!"

"I'm working on it, woman!"

The underbelly of the raider is clear now—just a few more seconds. Another shot on our ship.

"Hannibal!"

It's now or never. I make a few swipes, and the explosives ignite, and the raider explodes. Our ship is pushed but eventually rights itself. I walk up to the cockpit, and Kira is slouched in her seat.

"You okay?" I ask.

She swivels around in her seat to look at me and says, "You sure as hell took your time."

CHAPTER TWENTY-THREE

D UST, DIRT, AND GRIME SURROUND me. The sun beats down mercilessly on this godforsaken planet. Most everyone has left since the mines dried up, except for a few who couldn't afford the transport fare. A woman, whose dirt-caked face is streaked with tears, clutches my hand tightly, like the wind might blow me away. In front of us is a man dressed in full paladin regalia. He scans me, and his comm-tile glows green. The woman screams, falls to her knees, and clutches me around the waist.

Another man jerks me hard out of her arms and says, "It's time you pay your due to your family, Son."

I sit upright in my chair, gasping for breath. A hand at my shoulder causes me to jump.

"You okay?" asks an ebony-haired woman.

In a few seconds, I gain my bearings and remember where I am. I close my eyes and breathe deeply. I nod wordlessly then say, "Just a dream. Shouldn't you be sleeping?"

She leans on the console. "Shouldn't you be awake?"

I yawn and say, "Sorry about that." When she scrambles into my lap, I put my arms around her. "Seriously, you should be sleeping. We fixed all the damage best we could, so don't worry about that. We have maybe five hours before we arrive, and you need to get some rest because I'm sure it's not going to be a piece of cake once we get there."

She traces kisses starting at my ear down to my neck and asks, "What were you dreaming about?"

"It's a recurring one. I think it's when my parents sold me to the

Guild. I think my mother and father are in it. I don't really remember them. I don't even remember my real name."

She stops kissing and looks at me. "Seriously? So Hannibal Reece *isn't* your real name?"

I laugh and rub her side. "I guess as far as I remember, it is, but it's customary to rename foundlings so they forget all remnants of their former life. It's beaten into us that the Guild is our family and we are to be there for each other. Thing is, it was abundantly clear to me from early on they really never gave a shit about me or any of the other foundlings."

"*Foundlings.* That's a euphemism if ever I heard one. How old were you? You know, when you were sold."

"About seven, I think. I was the absolute oldest they'd take. I guess I scored incredibly high on their tests, so they gave my father a few hundred credits for me. From what I remember, my mother didn't want the deal to happen, but they were starving and thought it was best for everyone."

"You ever hear from them?"

"Nah, I can't even remember what planet I came from. It's no matter to me. I'm sure they're long dead by now."

Kira scoffs. "Why did you break away? I mean… Seems like the Guild is doing a pretty bang-up job of brainwashing hordes of drones who think the Guild is their family. Are you the only one who saw through all the bullshit?"

"No, about a year ago, a paladin about my age was publicly executed for indirectly getting the vaccine in the hands of Po. He was pretty vocal about his feelings on the Guild's vaccine distribution policies. He was stupid. There are a lot more smart paladins that have similar feelings—not just about the vaccine, but the direction of the Guild in general. However, they aren't as vocal." My hand moves from her side to her taut belly as I think of the life there now. My fingers flit gently over her stomach. I continue, "Maybe there's a part of me that remembers my mom, who loved me, and knows there should be better than the Guild. Or maybe I was just lucky to find you. The real irony is if Daimyo Corbin hadn't sent Tabor in to fuck up my run, then we wouldn't be together."

She laughs. "Remind me to send Tabor a thank-you letter for being such an utter fuckup."

I turn her so that her legs are straddling me and knead her lower back. She gives a satisfied sigh and moan. Her hips sway in response to my hands.

I laugh. "I'm sure that would go over rather well."

She leans down and feathers kisses on my lips.

I gently push her back. "Kira, you sure this is okay? I mean with…" I nod in the direction of her belly.

She smiles. "Yeah, silly, do you think married people go nine months without doing it? Just take it easy."

I pull her into me. "Kira, I need you."

"I need you too."

Both of us are nestled in the captain's chair, somewhere between asleep and awake. This will go down as one of the most perfect times in my life. Carefully, so as not to wake the sleeping woman, I sneak a look at my comm-tile to see our arrival time.

Hmm, another three hours. I slept longer than I wanted to.

I whisper into Kira's ear, "Hey, we're approaching Talus-9. We're going to have to throttle down."

She squirms and stretches. "Oh, okay." She sits up in my lap and leans to the console and pushes the requisite buttons, and we slow down. She yawns and rubs her eyes. "Let me check the long-range sensors to see if we have anything to prep for." Her face goes ashen, and her mouth draws down.

"What is it?"

"We're toast." She flips up the display so that it's floating in front of both of us.

My heart sinks. "Oh God."

CHAPTER TWENTY-FOUR

"**H**ANNIBAL, IT'S ABOUT TIME YOU made it here," Daimyo Raines says from the floating display. He looks Kira and me up and down with disgust. "Really, Hannibal, this is disgraceful. There's nothing this woman could give you that our courtesans couldn't. Turn the woman and cargo over to us, and you'll get a few demerits and time in the box—nothing you can't handle. Look, we all understand. A rather attractive woman, who is undoubtedly, uh… talented… tells you that you are the center of her universe, and you fall for her. The Guild is the only one that will always be here for you. She's using you. It's just another one of her cons, Hannibal."

Sitting to the side of Raines's video is a sensor display showing ten paladin Scimitars waiting for us outside Talus-9. We're no match for them. Just one of those Scimitars could take down that whole Hirabah raiding party we narrowly escaped. No way will we be able to break through.

I clench my jaw. "I'm not handing anyone or anything over. We have a contract with the Backics. So if you don't mind—"

"Hannibal! You are in over your head. That whore has you confused. We are the only family you have!" Daimyo Raines screams.

"She is not a whore! For the first time in my life, I'm seeing things more clearly. I'm done with the Guild."

"No one leaves the Guild!"

Kira shouts at the man, "Well, he just did!" She turns off the screen.

She paces back and forth in the cabin while running her hands through her hair. I look at the sensor display again. Their armor must have some kind of chink, something they haven't thought of. But I can think of nothing. The paladins never forget a thing. The Guild is a well-oiled machine intent on winning whatever challenge is set in front of it.

Kira plops down in her chair and pushes back on the throttle. "Okay, there's no need to panic just yet. I've slowed us down to buy us a bit more time. We need to think this through with a clear head." She takes a deep breath. "I assume if we turn tail and run—"

"They'll be on us faster than you can think."

"Exactly what I thought. I know they're waiting there just to fuck with us." She rubs her face and says to herself, "Think, Kira, think!" She looks at me. "Backics and The Independent Council are probably too busy to even mess with a comm from us, right?"

I nod. "I don't think Backics give a shit who gets the vaccine to them. If Raines and his crew get it to them, I'm sure they have deals worked out with other factions. They won't lift a finger to help."

Kira grumbles. "And the Independent Council can't help."

"Or can they?"

"Uh… No. *Independent* is exactly what it means. All the planets they represent are independent and poor and basically don't have a pot to piss in. Where the crap would they get money to raise an army in two hours?"

I wave my hand to dismiss her comment. "Kira, it's not like they have to be a formal thing. Do you have many clients in this system?"

"Oh yeah—plenty. Like five of the seven habitable planets here are terraformed, which means they need to outsource a lot of items from other systems. Plus, this is a particularly poor system that isn't really even on any Keepers' radar. So basically, no one cares enough to get them supplies except us independent transporters."

"For a large fee."

"Oh well, yeah. I mean, a girl's gotta drink."

I get a big smile on my face. "So how pissed do you think your customers would be if they found out the Guild is blocking their one good chance at getting the vaccine? And how quickly do you think that would get around? And how many people do you think might come help us deliver the vaccine?"

Her eyes get wide. "Holy shit, Reece. We're going to make great associates." Her face turns down. "Thing is… I don't want this to be a mass slaughter of innocents."

"I don't either. The Guild runs on propaganda just as much as the Keeper factions. If it gets around they're slaying a bunch of innocents who are protecting the vaccine promised to them, then their stock is going to plummet. We're trained to keep collateral damage to a minimum. Tell your contacts what's going on, that there's going to be a certain amount of danger going in, and we can give units to the first fifty that help us."

"On it." She says over a microphone, "This is Kira Dresden. Many of you know me as the transporter who visits here every few months to deliver your food, booze, and some other items you'd rather me not talk about on open waves. Today is a little different. My partner, Hannibal Reece, and I have negotiated a deal with the Backic faction and the Council of Independent Planets for several hundred units of vaccine. However, the Guild has seen their way to make a blockade at Talus-9, where we are supposed to deliver the items in the next two hours. If any of you feel the need to help us out, we'd sure be appreciative of it. And to show our appreciation, we have a unit of vaccine for the first fifty people who help us." She takes a breath and adds in a sincere tone, "I know a lot of you personally, and I know I can be a pain in the ass sometimes, but this is the real deal. We want to help, but we need your help to make this happen." She takes a moment, and her voice cracks. "Kira out."

CHAPTER TWENTY-FIVE

THE JOURNEY TO TALUS-9 FEELS like our own funeral procession. In the half hour since Kira made the call to the planets, we hear nary a response to her call. The closer we get, the faster my heart beats.

I look at Kira and say, "We have a little over an hour before our final approach, and it ain't lookin' so good."

She clenches her jaw. "Stupid scared assholes. If they want shit to change in their lives, then they need to stand up and do something about it and not constantly cower at the feet of the Keepers or the Guild. Fuck 'em all, anyway."

I take her hand. "We need to make preps. What weapons you got?"

She bobs up and down nervously and wipes a stray tear away. "Pretty much what you saw when the Hirabah raiding party struck us, and those assholes don't have near the firepower as the Scimitars in front of us." She looks away from me and breathes deeply. "I know we put patches on the damage the Hirabah did to us, but it's not going to hold when we start tussling with these guys."

"I know. I know. Focus on the mission, not the odds. I have a few more drones, and we can deploy those." I bring up the sensor display, and they are all still there. I point at the ships on the extreme outside flanks. "I'll take these guys out. I should have plenty of drones for that. Conservatively, that leaves six Scimitars for us to take out."

"Oh, that's all? Well then, shit, let me schedule my pedicure and prenatal massage."

"Kira! I'm trying to plan."

"I get it, hon. But… I think we need to seriously think of an exit strategy."

I knit my eyebrows. "What do you mean?"

"You've been a paladin for fifteen years. Right?"

"Yeah."

"In all the runs that you've been on, with odds like this, did your perp ever get away?" When I start to retort, she continues, "You told me I didn't want to know what happened to Po. You're right—I don't. But that's fixin' to happen to you, me, and our child now." She gets up from her seat and paces. "Very best-case scenario is they find out I'm pregnant, hold me in stasis or some shit until I have it, then take our child and raise it as a paladin, and you know what that's like. And you can damn sure bet it'll be hell for her since they'll make her pay for your supposed sins."

My heart sinks because I know she's right. Involuntary tears stream from my eye. She stands on her tiptoes and wipes them away and kisses me on the cheek.

"I'm not letting them take us," she says. "And the fuckin' vaccine can go up in flames for all I care. Fuck everyone in this system for not giving a damn."

I nod. "You're right. They're not taking my family. Our goal now is to cause the maximum amount of damage we can possibly do in the shortest amount of time."

She wipes her eyes and smiles. "Now… you're talkin'."

We both sit at the console and study the sensor map. "All right, I'm sure Raines and Corbin are probably the middle two ships leading the whole thing. I say our primary goals are those two fuckers."

"Agreed. Now, if we want to make it super special, we can overload my engine. It'll make a hell of spectacle and maybe take a few more ships at that."

It feels a little weird, talking about our own demise, but it's also oddly empowering, being in charge of my own fate for once. I just wish I had more time, more time with her.

I take Kira's hand, which is swirling about the console making preparations, and say, "For what it's worth, I'm not sorry that I met you that night. Thanks for giving me a taste of what life on the outside was like. I just wish we could've given that little one a chance."

She gets a half smile on her face. "Yeah, me too. And thanks for, ya know… liking me and stuff even though I'm an ass."

I give her kiss on the cheek. "It's easy to like you and stuff."

She gives me a sideways look.

"Sometimes."

"Okay, you done with the kissy-kissy stuff?"

"Quite."

"Good. We're less than an hour from the blockade. I've rigged this button"—she points at a red button on her console—"to overload the engine when pressed. One of us is going to have to press it right before impact. I'm sure it'll take out at least three surrounding ships if not more. They can all go fuck themselves and know the Dresden-Reece clan did it too."

As our ship nears the blockade, I hold Kira's hand, and we talk of our childhoods. Mostly, Kira does, for my childhood pretty much involved a never-ending boot camp. I'm amazed at how this woman, who can come off as just a two-bit con artist and thief, is actually one of the most poised, intelligent, confident people I've ever met in my life. I'm happy I got the chance to be a part of her world.

She looks at me and smiles. "Are you telling me you never played hide and seek?"

"Sorta, but we were given guns with live ammunition. No one ever got killed or anything, just tagged in a non-vital area so you didn't make the mistake of being found again."

She stares at me blankly for a few seconds then shakes her head. "Sooo, that's a no. Jeez, I can't believe all the childhood shit you missed out on." She takes my hand and puts her head on my shoulder. "I'm sorry."

A ring comes from her console, we both perk up, and she answers. The floating display is filled with Tabor's scarred face.

"I can't wait to get a piece of your woman, Hannibal. She must be a hell of a fuck."

Before I can say anything, Kira says, "Well, you bring the tweezers and magnifying glass, needle dick, and I'll be happy to satisfy your needs."

Enraged, Tabor yells, "You're a joke, Hannibal! We're going to take you down like an ordinary civilian, and we're going fuck up your woman. You'll be sorry—"

Kira gives Tabor the finger and turns off the screen. "He's lovely. We should have him over dinner."

I shake my head and look at the console. "Thirty minutes, hon. I guess this is it."

She waves me over to her seat. I move over, and she sits in my lap at the captain's seat, holding my hand. I guess there could be worse ways to go. Another ding comes from the console.

I mumble, "Tell Tabor to eat shit and die."

She sits up and inspects the console. "Gladly, but it's not Tabor."

"Who is it?"

She shrugs. "Not sure. Let me patch them through." After a few keystrokes, she says, "Identify yourself, star freighter."

"Heya, Kira, this is Bob Carro from Corgon-9. Don't suppose you remember getting us a shipment of medical supplies a few years back? But we really could use that vaccine. Offer still valid?"

She laughs. "Absolutely, Bob, but I don't have many more but you and me—" The console chimes again. "Hold on, Bob."

"Kira! Doll! This is Doris. Remember, you got antibiotic for my gentleman's club? We're in one hundred percent."

Kira answers, "O-Okay."

Another chime.

"Hey, lady! Am I too late? Really could use that vaccine."

"Nope, not at all."

One after another, the calls come in. All of them have been helped by Kira in some shape or form. All of them want the vaccine, not just for themselves but also for all in need. They are tired of the Keepers and the Guild having superiority over them. This is their one chance, their one moment to come together and stick it to The Man. For all her bravado and talk, Kira really has helped quite a few people over the years.

She looks at me and puts a hand to her mouth. "Hannibal, there's over thirty ships here."

"You're amazing." I get on the comms. "Thanks for joining us, friends. We're a little less than thirty minutes out. I know it may seem

In the Service of the Guild

daunting to go against a Paladin blockade like this, but know they are intimidated by your numbers too. We need to hold strong as a team. The more of us there are, the more likely they are to yield. Are you ready?"

Over the comms come whoops and hollers.

Kira rushes to me with a hug and looks up at me. "Hey, don't push that red button now. Okay?"

CHAPTER TWENTY-SIX

OUR CARAVAN HEADS TO THE great unknown. For once, I feel like we might have a chance. I say a prayer under my breath that these innocents will not be sacrificed. As we march forward, a message comes through, and Kira patches it in.

Daimyo Corbin's face is displayed. "Why are you bringing civilians into this, Reece?"

I respond, "Because they want their vaccine. They are tired of being screwed over by the Guild, the Keepers, everyone. They deserve their fair due too."

The daimyo's face turns a dark shade of pink as he stares me down. "This is unconscionable! You are a paladin first and foremost. You know better than to bring civilians into the mix."

I respond, "You brought them into the mix when you kept the vaccine from them. This is all on the Guild if a mass slaughter of innocents happens today."

Daimyo Raines's face replaces Corbin's. "Be reasonable, Reece. This is no way to end your career. We can talk this through."

I shake my head. "No, we can't. I'm done with you. The Guild. Every one of you. Let us through, or the Guild will be known as the biggest mass murderers of independent citizens ever."

Our ship rattles and shakes as a cacophony of buzzers and alarms sounds.

The fuzzy vidscreen displays Tabor's face smiling from ear to ear. "I'm going to take you down and find out what's so special about that woman."

Out the front window, I see a few shots fired from one of the

Independents at Tabor. They're no match for him, but it does give him pause.

He says to me, "Call off your flunkies before someone gets hurt."

"Can't do that, Tabor," Kira says.

Our ship is rocked again. This time, a few pieces of cargo are shaken loose from their tie-downs.

I can barely make out Raines's voice from our fuzzy display: "Tabor! Stand down!"

Tabor answers, "I have them, sir. Just one more—"

A mass of ships flock on Tabor and the daimyos, barraging them with fire. Alone, they wouldn't be a match, but together, they overwhelm the barricade.

Kira is at one with her ship, flying it through the melee, ignoring all the sounds and activities going on. I home in on Tabor's ship and give a few blasts just for fun.

Kira shakes her head. "Just had to get those in, didn't you?"

"Of course."

Our ship is hurtling closer to the planet. The Guild seems to be too preoccupied with incoming Independents to mess with us.

Kira's brow furrows in worry. "We're coming in rather hot to hit atmo. It's going to be tough. Buckle up and say a prayer."

In an instant, my body feels like it's been hit by a massive object. The sky goes from black to a brilliant blue. We're skidding out of control. Kira's face is sweating and contorting as she tries like hell to get her ship under control.

She screams, "C'mon, you bitch! You can do this. Don't let me down." As the ship heats up, skids, and sways, Kira braces herself against the seat and tugs on the controls with all her might. "I'm not going down like this! I can land a ship!"

Suddenly, a modern city with a few pristine high-rises comes into sight. We've made it. But we're still coming in awfully fast.

"Kira, uh, I'm not one to tell you how to fly, but…"

Her gaze is focused ahead as she clenches her jaw. "Okay then, don't. I got this, Hannibal."

The ground quickly comes to meet us, and the cargo box that was jarred loose flies through the air to land right on Kira, slamming her body into the console. She falls onto the ground, the box landing on top of her. I take the controls and make the final landing sequence.

The ship is dark and filled with smoke and flashing lights. Immediately, I run to Kira's side and shove the box off her. A trickle of blood streams from her mouth, and more blood is pooled at her head. I breathe deeply and remind myself that head wounds always look worse than they are. I pat her cheek.

"Kira, hon, wake up. You did a great job. You got us on the ground. C'mon. Let's go."

Her body is limp and unresponsive. I tear my shirt and put it to the wound on her head to try to stop the bleeding.

No, no, this is not happening. Okay, Reece, you need to contact the Independent Council. If you don't get the shipment to them, all of this will be for naught.

I make a few swipes to my comm-tile and speak. "To Backic and Independent Council, the shipment of vaccine is here approximately"—I check my tile—"an hour before the agreed-on time per our contract. I am sending coordinates now. Please consider us in agreement of our contract. Also, please send medical personnel immediately."

A voice comes over the comms. "This is Helena Rey. Transmission received. Personnel will be there in minutes."

Kira gives a barely audible moan.

I take her hand. "Kira, listen to me. They will be here in a few minutes. Don't give up, okay?"

Her eyes barely open. "Jeez, I feel like shit." She gives me a sneaky smile then asks, "What the hell'd you do to my ship, Reece?"

I laugh. "I hardly think I'm totally to blame for this."

She starts to laugh, then her face turns down, and her hand goes to her belly. "I don't have a good feeling about this."

CHAPTER TWENTY-SEVEN

THE SMELL OF DISINFECTANT BURNS my nose as I sit by Kira's bedside in the med clinic. We're in a tiny stark-white private room that I can almost reach both sides of if I stretch far enough. One of Kira's arms is webbed in a black cast, and she has it propped up on her chest. With her one good hand, she fiddles with the bandage on her head then her IV.

"Will you cut that out," I say to her. "You're going to screw something up."

"No, I'm not. Where is the doc? They said an hour ago she'd be here in fifteen minutes. It can only be bad news."

"It's not bad news."

"Did they tell you how the baby was?"

My stomach falls, but I try not to let the stress show on the outside. "Kira, there were a lot of people who came in with injuries after us. It's a good thing the Guild called it off when they did because there would be a lot more here. I'm sure they're just attending to those people. Besides, they wouldn't tell me how she was without you since they don't know I'm the father." I take her hand and say, "Just try to relax, hon."

Her lip quivers when she says, "They never tell you the bad news right away. They want to check and make sure it's true before they tell you. If they were sure, they'd just say, 'Hey, everything's fine.' Hannibal, it's not good."

The door opens, and a statuesque blonde appears, wearing a crisp black suit and perfectly coifed hair. As she smiles, her blue eyes sparkle. "Job well done, you two."

Kira sneers and asks, "And you would be...?"

The blond woman extends her hand, which Kira takes hesitantly. She says, "Helena Rey. I was Hannibal's contact with the Backic faction. I authorized the terms, and I'm impressed with how you were able to negotiate better terms than we originally agreed on."

Kira eyes her up and down, not losing that look somewhere between disgust and murderous tendency, mostly toward me. "You're his contact?"

Helena nods and smiles. Kira looks at me, and my body goes numb.

She continues, "Mmm... I see. So what's the deal? You guys protecting us or what?"

"Absolutely. True to our terms, we will be calling off any and all hits on you and Paladin Reece."

I hold up my hand and stop her. "It's just Hannibal Reece now, ma'am."

She gives a little chuckle. "Oh, you always were so polite."

I don't dare to look at Kira now, but the viselike grip she has my hand in tells me exactly what she's thinking.

Helena starts again. "Paladin or not, we will not be pursuing any retribution from you or your..." She looks at Kira and sighs. "Associate. We consider all deals met. We will strongly suggest that the Guild let you go your way, Mr. Reece. I'm sure they will leave you two alone for the time being as your faces are all over every last news feed as the saviors of the Independent Council of Planets." She practically rolls her eyes at that last statement. "Even the Guild knows when to cut their losses."

Kira eyes Helena for a few seconds and says, "I expect we're going to get this in writing."

"You are very shrewd. My assistant is sending documents to your comm-tiles that certify what I just said now. I'll leave you two to um... whatever it is you were doing. We may be contacting you in the future for other business." She starts for the door but stops just short of opening it and turns toward us. "It's a shame we weren't able to complete our contract, Hannibal, but she must be pretty special for you to risk everything for."

The door closes behind her, and I simultaneously yank my hand from Kira's grip. "Ow! Damn! What the hell, Kira?"

She narrows her eyes and asks, "Was that who you were matched with?"

"Yes, but hey, it saved our asses."

"Yeah, I can't believe you gave up a filthy-rich six-foot blonde for me."

I lean over to her bed and kiss her forehead. "Eh, she's got nothing on you—"

The creaking of the door interrupts us, and two daimyos caked with soot and char come barging through the door, staring me down.

Raines says between clenched teeth, "What the fuck is the meaning of this, Reece? Say goodbye to the whore, and let's go. You have an appointment with the elders."

I take Kira's hand and shake my head. "*No!* I am no longer one of you." I look at Kira, who gives me a nod of confidence. "She is my family now."

Corbin growls, "You can't leave the Guild. No one leaves the Guild. We will find you and—"

Kira pipes up. "Listen, we've struck a deal with the Backic faction, and we're under their protection. Also, I'm sure in a few hours, the beautiful mugs of yours truly and Hannibal are going to be on every flippin' news outlet as the ones who have made the vaccine available to all the poor Independents. So you kill me or Hannibal, then it's going to look pretty bad and petty."

Both the men stare down Kira, and Corbin is about to retort when a nurse comes barging in. She looks at the two men. "What are you doing in here? She's only authorized one visitor, and that is her partner there."

Kira puts a hand to her head and feigns a weak voice. "Can you please get them out of here? I don't feel so good. I'm so tired."

The nurse swats the men. "Shoo! Get on outta here."

Corbin and Raines file out, but Corbin looks over his shoulder and says to me, "This is isn't the last you've heard from the Guild."

Kira says, "Please get them out of here. I... I think I'm going to faint."

Once the men are out of the room, I look at Kira. "Nice performance."

"I thought so." She's silent for a second then says, "Hannibal, I know something's wrong." She puts her good hand to her belly.

"Shut up. Let's talk about something else. So now that the contract's signed, sealed, and delivered, what are we going to do?"

She shrugs and looks down. "I don't know. I guess it depends on... ya know."

"Let's assume everything is okay. Then what?"

She takes a big breath. "Welp, I assume you need to go look for gainful employment somewhere because I'm pretty sure your old employer isn't taking you back. I was serious about forming your own collective of mercs. You have a vision. You could give those assholes at the Guild a run for their money. I believe in you, Hannibal."

"Kira, the only thing I was ever good at was taking orders."

"Not true. You are smart—too smart and too good to be with them. They knew it, and that's why they put the screws down on you. Here's your chance. Go do something wonderful and spectacular. Take this opportunity and—"

She's stopped by a woman in a lab coat entering the room. Kira squeezes my hand and swallows hard. I give her an encouraging smile. The woman smiles, but I can't really make out if it's an I'm-sorry smile or a professional-courtesy smile.

"Ms. Dresden, I have your results." She looks at me, a question whether she should go on with me in the room. When Kira nods, the doctor continues. "I've reviewed all your scans. Obviously, your arm is broken. Our scans show that your concussion is minor, but still, don't dismiss it, and take it easy for the next few weeks." She fiddles with her comm-tile, presumably to look at some notes. She stops, and her eyes go wide. "Oh my, I'm sorry—"

My heart stops, and my body goes cold. I squeeze Kira's hand more tightly.

"They didn't tell me you were expecting. I would've told you to start off with: your baby is fine. I'm so sorry that got buried in the notes."

Kira starts to cry, and I stand to take her in my arms.

The doctor continues, "It was a hell of a lot of trauma, so I want you to stay here for two more days just so we can monitor you and the baby, but from these scans I'm looking at now, it looks like everything will be fine. I am going to recommend that you take it easy for the next week, though. You need to get better nutrition and take prenatal vitamins."

Kira is sobbing, unable to answer.

I say in her stead, "Will do, ma'am."

The doctor exits the room, and I look back at Kira. "I told ya so. You know our kid has to be tough."

"Yeah, I guess so. But I still meant what I said. You need to go find yourself. You've been tied to the Guild for your whole life. You don't need to run straight to me bossing you around. You're a smart guy, Hannibal. I'm pretty sure I can talk the indies into giving me a reduced or free rate on my repairs. I know how to get a hold of you if I need you."

"Kira, you're right. At some point, I do need to find myself, but I'm not leaving you and that kid alone to take crazy-ass jobs by yourself. I'm not leaving you alone to… give her to your cousin. I'll be shacking up with you until the nugget is here. After it's all said and done, then we can see where the rest of our lives take us. Deal?"

She laughs. "Deal."

CHAPTER TWENTY-EIGHT

THE HUM OF GRAV-STABILIZERS FILLS my spartan quarters. I click through a few reports on my floating display as I lean back in my squeaking chair, trying to take myself from the monotony of the job lying in front of me.

Almost like a savior, my comm-tile buzzes with an incoming encrypted message:

HAPPY THIRD BIRTHDAY, LYVIA KIRECE BAX-DUPREE.

I click on the message and swipe on it so that it floats in the air. Displayed is a little girl with a cherry-red birthmark on her chin and ebony hair in pigtails with cake smeared all over her face. In another picture, she is between her dads with her hands in the air in pure joy. Another picture shows her sleeping peacefully on a couch, snuggling a new educational bot that her dads, Kira, and I chipped in for. She is safe and happy.

I finally did something right.

Just like previous years at this time, the pictures cause the memories to flood in. The months spent with Kira pregnant and emotional on her ship made the Crucible look like a cakewalk. In true Kira fashion, she worked up to the due date, underestimating the time it would take to get to a med facility, making me responsible for delivering that little nugget into this world. Holding her and looking into her eyes was the best thing I ever did in this world. And if staying with Kira made the Crucible look like a cakewalk, then giving the baby to Kira's cousin, Mark Bax, made it look like a stay in heaven. My heart broke, and my world was shattered, but Kira and I knew it was for the best. Kira was right—I needed to find my way in the world, and fortunately, I found some very talented mercs that were willing to take a chance on a former paladin and a risky venture.

Before I have time to go down memory lane too far, a voice comes through the door to my quarters.

"Hannibal, your old lady's on Comm One..."

I bark out, "My what?"

"Uh, sorry, sir. Ms. Dresden wants to speak to you."

"Patch her through."

A woman with an ebony ponytail is displayed. "You get the pics?"

"Yup. Good thing she looks like you. I think she might like the bot."

"I hope so. Set me back some hefty credits." Her smile tells me she doesn't give a damn about the credits. She starts again. "Hey, I got a line on a run. You want the details?"

"Absolutely. When you coming to see me again, woman? I haven't seen you in weeks."

She grins from ear to ear. "Gotta get this one job in first, and I'm headed home. Oh, and hey, the damn Guild is hot and heavy in the Vega system. I'd stay the hell away if I were you until things cool down."

"Aw, you care."

"Whatever."

The screen goes black, and I exit my quarters and bellow as I walk through the hallways, "All right, you pukes! Time for quarters in the mess area. We got a run to make!"

THE END... for now

ACKNOWLEDGEMENTS

Thank you to my husband for reading an extremely early draft of this and giving me encouragement to finish. You'll never know what it means to me to have someone read early drafts and encourage me to press on even through the rough patches.

Thank you a zillion million times to Jennifer Scroggins for the "Words with Friends Game" that resulted in an awesome back of the book blurb. Man, how I hate writing these things.

Thank you to fans who keep reading and actually asking for more books. That is a huge motivator to know there are multiple people out there who actually like what you wrote.

ABOUT THE AUTHOR

Paige Daniels is a science fiction author living in the middle of a corn patch somewhere in the American Midwest. Her previous series is the cyberpunk action adventure series, NON-COMPLIANCE. She is also the co-editor of BRAVE NEW GIRLS, a young adult sci-fi anthology, which aims to inspire the next generation of STEM talent.

Paige has her B.S. in Physics and Electrical Engineering and an M.S. in Systems Engineering. When she isn't working her 9-5 job or writing she manages a hobby farm with her delightful husband and two kids.

You can find her at:
www.nerdypaige.com
www.facebook/paigedanielsauthor.com

Made in the USA
Monee, IL
31 October 2020